I0708102

# The emergence of writing from Akkadian to Aramaic (Syriac, Arabic, Hebrew, Mandaic), Sabaean, and Geezy

Nazar H. Dayraya

Book name: The Emergence of Writing from Akkadian
to Aramaic Sabaean, and Geezy
Author name: Nazar Hana Alderaya
Cover designer: Ashure Nazar
Publisher: Timescape Books

# TABLE OF CONTENTS

# Chapter 1
# From cuneiform to the alphabet

Experts are still struggling to understand how writing evolved[1], but one theory, on display at the Oriental Institute exhibition, places the final stage of pictorial writing and the emergence of the new form in 3400 BC, when the Sumerians first began using clay envelopes containing small clay balls. Sealed inside Archaeologists assume that it was sent with the goods being delivered; the recipients will open it and make sure that the number of dues matches the number of clay tokens.

Although there are discussions regarding the origin of this Sumerian writing, most opinions focus on the Iraqi

DEVELOPMENT OF WRITING IN THE ANCIENT WORLD[1]
https://africame.factsanddetails.com/article/entry-63.html

city of Uruk - south of Babylon, which was characterized by rapid urbanization and population growth.

A group of writings was discovered in Uruk in 1924 by a group of German archaeologists led by Julius Jordan[2], where these texts were found in the Fourth Uruk layer on approximately 1000 texts, these texts contain many tangible pictorial images and are dated between 4100 and 3800 BC.

Where the simplest form of writing on cylinder seals was found, and it contains the distinctive personal signs of the ancient Sumerians, scholars argue that this writing did not appear complete in the fourth millennium BC.

In other words, the art of writing in Mesopotamia can be traced back to before this date[3], that is, to the counting system in the eighth millennium BC using clay symbols of multiple shapes.

Researcher Denise Schmandt Besserat[4] from the University of Texas says: "The direct antecedents of

---

DEVELOPMENT OF WRITING IN THE ANCIENT WORLD[22]
https://africame.factsanddetails.com/article/entry-63.html
 The Evolution of Writing[3]
**Published in** James Wright, ed., INTERNATIONAL ENCYCLOPEDIA OF SOCIAL AND BEHAVIORAL SCIENCES, Elsevier, 2014
https://sites.utexas.edu/dsb/tokens/the-evolution-of-writing/
[4] Denis Chamant-Bésserat, Briscoe Center for American History, University of Texas at Austin, January 23, 2014

writing in Mesopotamia were a recording device consisting of clay symbols of multiple shapes. Many artifacts were found, most of which were geometric shapes such as cones, discs, cylinders, and oval shapes. In archaeological sites dating back to 8000-3000 BC.

In general, we say that the origins of writing in Sumer are generally attributed to the beginning of the pottery phase in the Neolithic period, when special writing was used to record specific livestock or transactions and this writing was initially printed on the surface of round clay balls which were stored in clay envelopes.

And after that these balls were then gradually replaced by flat disks, on which writing was recorded with a stylus.

According to many sources, writing was first invented in Uruk (southern Iraq) at the end of the fourth millennium BC, and soon after appeared in various parts of the Near East, where four more or less independent inventions are recognized:

1- Mesopotamia (ca. 3400–3100 BC).

2- Egypt (ca. 3250 BC).

3- China (ca. 1400-1200 BC).

4- Central America around 600-500 BC, and others date the period of the emergence of the art of writing in the Maya civilization around 250-900 BC.

---

Sumerian cuneiform and Egyptian hieroglyphics are generally considered among the oldest examples of true writing systems, and some argue that the proto-Elamite script, which was deciphered on November 27, 2020, by the French archaeologist François Desset[5], appeared as early as 3100 BC. It is believed that writing in it developed into the Elamite script by the third millennium and was then replaced by the Elamite cuneiform script, emerging from Akkadian.

Regarding Egyptian hieroglyphics, scholars point to very early differences with Sumerian cuneiform "in structure and style," meaning the two systems may have developed independently.

The Egyptians, like the Sumerians, were among the first people to develop a writing system.

Haifa Ali - Al-Baath Weekly Newspaper - Issue 17, Wednesday, December [5] 16, 2020

Their writing system was very different from the one we use today.

Instead of alphabet letters, they used pictures and symbols[6] that we call "hieroglyphics, the word "hieroglyphs" is a Greek word that means "sacred writing." This is an indication that the ancient Egyptians believed that knowledge of writing was something granted by Thoth, the god of knowledge.

Despite what researcher Geoffrey Sampson[7] stated; Egyptian hieroglyphics "came into existence shortly after Sumerian writing, and may have been invented under the influence of the

Narmer stela 3100 BC hieroglyphics and writing

latter," and that "it is possible that the written language was brought to Egypt from Sumerian Mesopotamia. This

DEVELOPMENT OF WRITING IN THE ANCIENT WORLD[6]
https://africame.factsanddetails.com/article/entry-63.html
[7] History of writing
From Wikipedia, the free encyclopedia
https://en.wikipedia.org/wiki/History_of_writing#Writing_materisls

is due to the presence of important relationships between the two regions.

However, because there is no direct evidence of the transfer of writing from Sumerian to Egyptian[8], a final determination has not been reached regarding the origin of hieroglyphic writing in ancient Egypt, as some saw that the evidence for this direct influence is still weak and that it can also be considered a very credible argument in support of independent development to write in Egypt.

Uruk signs represent the first stage of writing in Mesopotamia (pottery stage 3100-3350 BC)

However, most linguists agree that the Sumerians were the first to know writing in human history, more than

---

[8] History of writing
From Wikipedia, the free
encyclopediahttps://en.wikipedia.org/wiki/History_of_writing#Writing_materi
als

5,650 years ago, and this writing was derived from pictographic writing that came from them.

Sumerian writing went through several evolutionary stages, the motive behind which was to keep pace with the development of society and the social life of the population, because it, that is, writing, is the means and tool through which their ideas are recorded and transmitted, their incomes and expenses are documented, as well as their rights and transactions are confirmed and preserved from loss, as in the following figure, which describes the amount of barley needed to cultivate the field. It dates back to the Uruk period 3100 BC.

As well as in the following figure, which dates back to the Uruk period of 3200 BC.

In the half of the fourth millennium BC, the inhabitants of Mesopotamia began writing signs on wet clay, which was the first writing system in the world. The text is known as cuneiform (from the Latin word "wedge" cuneus), and this name refers to the appearance of signs in the form of a wedge, or diagrams. , which is designed with a reed pen.

The cuneiform script was invented to represent the Sumerian language, and the Akkadians later developed the cuneiform script to make it a little easier to write in a wide range of languages throughout the ancient world of the East, including Akkadian, Eblaite, Elamite, Hittite, Hurrian, Old Persian, And Urarty. Cuneiform writing remained in use alongside Aramaic until the late first century BC. Others go until the late first century AD due to the use of clay as the main medium for writing instead of perishable materials such as papyrus.

Therefore, Mesopotamia was considered one of the best-documented civilizations before the Industrial Revolution.

The number of symbols was reduced from about 900 in the ancient text to about 600, and at some point, most likely in the third millennium BC[9]. As in the table below[10] :

---

[9] T H E O R I E N T A L I N S T I T U T E NO. 207 FALL 2010 © THE ORIENTAL INSTITUTE OF THE UNIVERSITY OF CHICAGThe Origins of Writing in MesopotamiaChristopher Woods
https://www.academia.edu/16554752/The_Origins_of_Writing_in_Mesopota mia?email_work_card=thumbnail
[10] Jerrold Cooper, "Babylonian Beginnings: The Origins of the Cuneiform ",Writing System in Comparative Perspective
The Origins of Writing in Mesopotamia
Christopher Woods

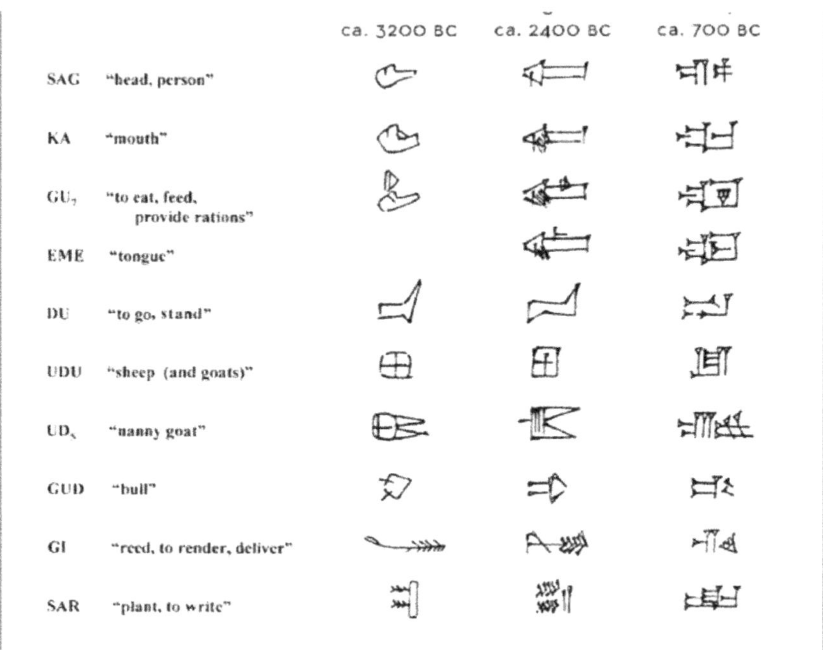


تطور العلامات المسمارية

However, this method was difficult and complex, as scholars counted approximately 550 symbols (syllables) in addition to other signs (movements) that give one symbol several meanings[11], which necessitated finding another easier and simpler way of writing.

Since the middle of the second millennium, there have been multiple attempts to invent a simpler written form. The principle of these new writing systems was to neglect formal signs and reduce hundreds of syllabic signs to a manageable number. This means instead of having

---

[11] D. Fawzi Rashid / Grammar of the Sumerian Language - Baghdad 1972, p. 17

separate syllabic signs, as is the case in Babylonian cuneiform writing, for audio clips such as:

(ME, MAY, MO, AM, YAM, WAM)[12]

The Arameans created a single sign that could perform all of these syllables, and where each symbol or image in it represented a sound output instead of the syllable.

The transition from cuneiform to the alphabet in the ancient Near East took place over several centuries. In the seventh century BC, the Assyrian kings were still dictating their decrees to two scribes. The first was writing in the Akkadian language and cuneiform script on a clay tablet. The second was writing in the Aramaic alphabet on a clay tablet or a scroll of papyrus.

Phoenician merchants who settled on the coast of present-day Syria and Lebanon played an important role in spreading the alphabet. In particular, they transferred their alphabetic system to Greece, perhaps as early as 800 BC, or even earlier.

Alphabetic writing, which is considered the first beginning of several writings, is a sequence of letters according to sound, and it has also passed through several stages throughout the ages which:

---

The Aramaic language and ancient libraries / Harry Sacks - Translated by: [12]
Saeed Al-Ghanimi
https://annabaa.org/arabic/arts/5876

1- Ugaritic alphabet: It is one of the first alphabets, and it was contemporary with the Akkadian and Sumerian languages. It was used more than 3,500 years ago (1,500 BC) in Syria. It consists of 30 letters according to the alphabet system and was written from left to right. As shown below[13]:

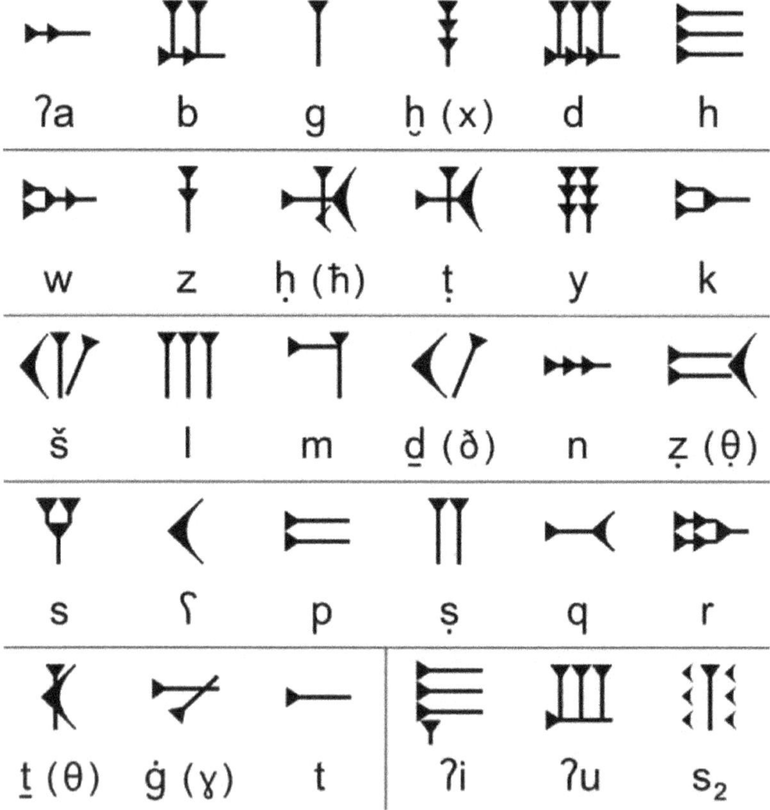


2- The Phoenician alphabet: It is one of the ancient alphabetical writings after the Ugaritic alphabet, dating back to 3,300 years ago. Inscriptions and writings of it were found in the Byblos region - Lebanon, dating back

---

[13] https://ar.wikipedia.org/wiki

to before the tenth century BC. It turned out to be an advanced form of syllabic writing to shorten the number of signs used from 30 signs to 22. It was written from right to left, as its letters were easier than the letters of the Ugaritic language. Dr. Philip Hitti says about it[14]:

(There is no doubt that the greatest blessing bestowed by the Phoenicians on human civilization was the discovery of the letter. The Phoenicians were the first people to use pure alphabets in writing. In addition to this, they were the transmitters and publishers of this letter in the civilized world at that time). As shown in the figure below.

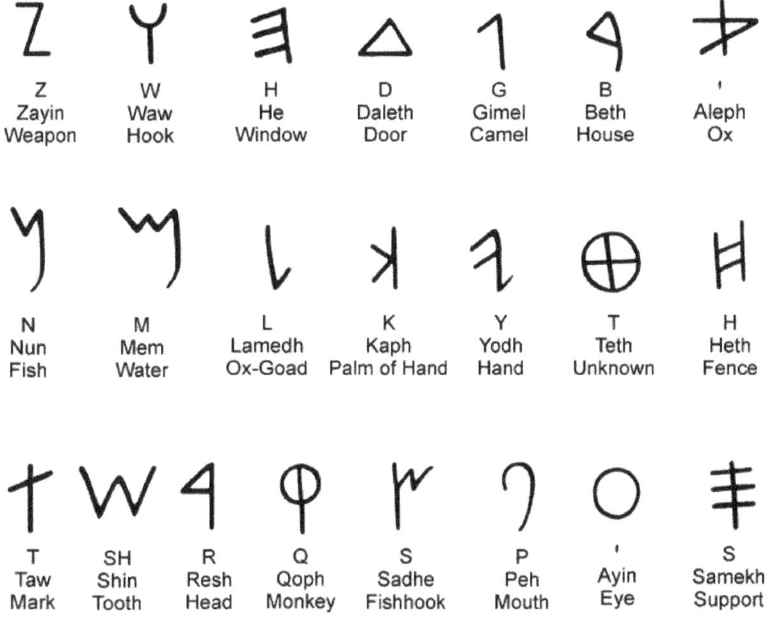


---

[14] Father Emile Edde / Statements of historians and archaeologists - from the Internet

3- Aramaic alphabet: appeared about 3000 years ago in Syria and Iraq. This writing was practiced by many civilizations and nations, such as the Assyrians, Chaldeans, and Achaemenids. It is considered the first alphabetic writing whose letters began to connect at a later stage, and it is still a spoken language in the region. It contains 22 letters.

It had several dialects, what remains of it:

1- Arabic: It is widely used in Arab countries and diaspora countries.

2- Syriac: It is used to a limited extent in Iraq, Iran, Turkey, Syria, Lebanon, Palestine, India, and the countries of the diaspora.

3- Hebrew: It is used in Israel and diaspora countries.

4- Mandaic: It is used within a specific scope in Iraq and diaspora countries.

5- The dialects of Maaloula, Jabadeen, and Bakhma (three villages on the outskirts of Damascus, (the first is Christian and the second and third are Islamic).

> Maaloula is one of the few remaining communities whose people still speak the Western Aramaic dialect and it was transmitted orally for generations until 2006 when the Aramaic Language Institute was established there by the University of Damascus to teach courses to keep the language alive.

4- The Sabaean and Geez group: Researchers believe that writing in the southern Arabian Peninsula, Abyssinia, and Somalia dates back to the ninth and perhaps the tenth century BC, in light of the discovered inscriptions, which are called the Musnad script in the Arabian Peninsula and Somalia, and the Musnad and Gezi script in both Eritrea and Ethiopia.

# Geez alphabet

| U | ʌ | ሐ | መ | ሠ | ረ | ሰ | ቀ | በ |
|---|---|---|---|---|---|---|---|---|
| hoy | lawe | ḥawṭ | may | sawt | re's | śat | ḳaf | bet |
| h | l | ḥ | m | ś/ḍ | r | s | ḳ | b |
| [h] | [l] | [ħ] | [m] | [ɬ'] | [r] | [s] | [k'] | [b] |

| ተ | ነ | ኀ | አ | ከ | ወ | ዐ | ዘ | የ |
|---|---|---|---|---|---|---|---|---|
| tawe | ḥarm | nahas | 'alf | kaf | wawe | 'ayn | zay | yaman |
| t | ḫ | n | ' | k | w | ʻ | z | y |
| [t] | [χ] | [n] | [ʕ] | [k] | [w] | [ʔ] | [z] | [j] |

| ደ | ገ | ጠ | ጰ | ጸ | ፀ | ፈ | ፐ |
|---|---|---|---|---|---|---|---|
| dant | gaml | ṭayt | pait | ṣaday | ḍappa | af | psa |
| d | g | ṭ | p̣ | ṣ | ḍ/ś | f | p |
| [d] | [g] | [t'] | [p'] | [t͡s'] | [t͡ɬ'/ɬ'] | [f] | [p] |

# Sabaean alphabet

# Chapter 2
# Semitic designation

Linguists have named a linguistic group that includes the peoples whose speakers currently live in the Middle East, North and East Africa, specifically (Syria, Iraq, Arabian Peninsula, Yemen, Ethiopia, and Eritrea).

It includes the languages Akkadian (with its Ashorian and Babylonian branches), Canaanite, Ugaritic, Phoenician, Aramaic, Hebrew, Mandaic, Syriac, Arabic, Sabaean, and Geez, with its branches (Amharic and Tigrinya) being Semitic, and its peoples being Semitic.

The first to give the name (Semitic Languages) to this family; He is the German historian and linguist August Ludwig von Schlzer. Some call him Schultz (1735 - 1809), a member of the German Göttingen School of History, in 1781 AD, after Shem, son of Noah, based on the book of the Old Testament, because this group shares common characteristics.

However, his German colleague Johann Gottfried Eichhorn (1752-1827), a member of the school, used the term "Semitic" to refer to the group (Hebrew, Arabic, and Syriac Aramaic) that have similarities, based on the comparative analysis of the languages (Hebrew, Arabic, and Syriac Aramaic) published by the French orientalist Guillaume. Postel (1510-1581) in 1538 in Latin, After him, the orientalist Heub Ludolf (1625 - 1704), a German linguist, who is considered the first and most famous person to be interested in the Geez language, described it through the relationship that arose between him and a Gregorian monk from Ethiopia - from the regions of the Amhara tribe, and through this relationship, he obtained from the monk comprehensive knowledge. About the Geez language, as it became clear to him that there were similarities between these three languages and the Geez language. However, none of the researchers at that time called this group "Semitic."

I say that if it was necessary to rely on the Old Testament, Schlözer had to use the Babylonian name (Akkadian / Aramaic), because the Old Testament defines the word Babylon in the sense of confusion of languages, that is, there was one language during the construction of the Tower of Babel, and God punished those working in the construction by confusing their languages so that they can't understand each other in order to complete their tower project.

 This means that there was one language used in Babylon and the region, whether Akkadian or Aramaic, during the writing of the Old Testament, and then divided into several languages.

After that, and based on the theory put forward by some orientalists, considering that all peoples (Akkadians, Assyrians, Chaldeans, and Arameans) were displaced from the Arabian Peninsula, this language was called Al-Jazariyah. However, they were not able to prove this, as the monuments found in Mesopotamia are the oldest and did not Evidence of this has been found on the island, so I do not agree with this theory either. I think it is more correct to call this group Aramaic until the commonality with Akkadian is explained. After that, we can move to the Akkadian name, which is more correct.

Because Aramaic became for a period the language of the empires (Assyrian, Chaldean, and Achaemenid) and because of the expansion of the influence and rule of these empires in the region, the Aramaic writing was transmitted through them to these countries whose people were called Semites.

Meaning that the language used, which facilitated the process of transfer and coexistence among them, was a mixture of Akkadian and Aramaic and their cross-fertilization with local languages. Otherwise, how can I read and translate the inscriptions found in Somalia, Eritrea, Ethiopia, Yemen, and Saudi Arabia, despite them being written in another script, in addition to the inscriptions in the Levant, Iraq, Palestine, Jordan, and perhaps later other inscriptions in the Gulf States? Father Emil Adah says[15]:

(All alphabets worthy of this name, whether ancient or modern, are related, to some extent, to the Canaanite-Phoenician alphabet. The Arameans of Syria and Mesopotamia, who transferred their language to this alphabet, contributed to its spread through their trade, as far as China and the Arab countries. Thanks to the alphabet, the Aramaic language occupied the position of Babylonian Akkadian as a diplomatic and commercial

---

[15] Father Emile Edde / Statements of historians and archaeologists - from the Internet

language in the Eastern Mediterranean, and then as a national language throughout the Fertile Crescent.)

In this study, we will try to focus on the emergence of the Aramaic and Sabaean Geezian alphabets.

# Chapter 3

# The emergence of alphabets

# First: The emergence of the Aramaic alphabet

Although there is no final agreement on when and where alphabetic writing appeared, a group of researchers believe that its first emergence must have occurred in Syria and Phoenicia, which were the meeting places of the two civilizations (Mesopotamia and Egypt), and this alphabet consisted of 22 letters.

Writer Sabatino Moscati says[16]:

(One of the greatest glories of the Phoenicians, and perhaps the greatest of all, is that they spread the alphabet in the countries of the Mediterranean. There is absolutely no doubt that the Phoenicians taught Greece the alphabet, just as the Phoenicians and Greece introduced this writing to the West...).

There is evidence indicating its appearance, including the Obelisk of Mesha, King of Moab, which was found east of the Dead Sea. The date of its writing dates back to the middle of the ninth century BC. It was written by King Mesha, the king of the Moabite Kingdom, a kingdom

---

[16] Father Emile Edde / Statements of historians and archaeologists - from the Internet

whose star shone during the ninth century BC in central Jordan. This obelisk is one of the oldest and longest historical obelisks discovered in the Levant, in which the king commemorates his victories over the Children of Israel in the year 850 BC. The writing says, according to its publishers[17]:

{Am Mesha, son of Chemosh [ît], king of Moab, the Dibonite? My father ruled over Moab for thirty years, and I ruled after my father. I made this high place for Chemosh in Qerihoh, a *high-place of salvation*, for he saved me from all the kings and made me enjoy the sight of my enemies. Om-ri, king of Israel, oppressed Moab for a long time because Chemosh was angry with (6) His country. His son succeeded him, and he also declared: "I will oppress Moab." In my days, he declared thus, but I enjoyed his view and that of his house: Israel was destroyed forever. Omri had taken possession of the land of Madaba, and he dwelt in it (during) his days and, *(during) half* of *my* days, his sons, forty years, but Chemosh restored it during my days. I built Baal-Meon, and I made a reservoir in it; I built Kiriathain. The men of Gad dwelt in the land of Atarot from ancient times, and the king of Israel had built Atarot, but I fought against the city and took it; I killed the entire population. The city belonged to Chemosh and to Moab, and I brought back from there the hearth-altar of his Well-Beloved, and I installed it before Chemosh in my capital. I settled there the men of Sharon and the men of Maharat. Chemosh said to me: "Go, take Nebo from Israel!" I went

---

[17] What Does the Mesha Stele Say?/ André Lemaire  November 18, 2022 https://www.biblicalarchaeology.org/daily/biblical-artifacts/inscriptions/what-does-the-mesha-stele-say/

in the night, and I fought there from dawn until noon; I took it and killed everyone: seven thousand men, boys, women, [daughters, and pregnant women because I devoted it to Ashtar Chemosh. I took from there, the hear [Th] altars of Yahweh, and I brought them before Chemosh. The king of Israel had built Yahaz, and he lived there while fighting against me, but Chemosh drove him out before me; I took two hundred men of Moab, all its divisions, and I led them against Yahaz; I took it to add it to Dibon. I built Qerihoh: the wall of its parks and the wall of the citadel; I built its gates, its towers, and a royal palace. I made the retaining walls of the water reservoir within the city. There had not been a cistern within the city, in Qerihoh, and I said to all the people: "Build for you a cistern, each one in his house!" I had Qerihoh's ditches dug by Israelite prisoners. I built Aroer and made the road in the Arnon.

I (re)built Beth-Bamoth because it had been destroyed. I (re)built Bezer because it was in ruins. The men of Dibon (were) fitted out for war because all Dibon (is my) guard. I ruled over hundreds of cities that I added to the land. I built [the temple of Madaba, the temple of Diblaten, and the temple of Baal-Meon. I transported there […] the small cattle of the land. The House of David dwelt in Horonain [……] and Chemosh said to me: "Go down, fight against Horonain!" I went down, [fought against the city and took it.] Chemosh restored it in my days, and I made up ten.

Other Aramaic inscriptions found in Zanjerli in Syria date back to the ninth and eighth centuries BC.

Many researchers agree that the Aramaic alphabet (derived from Phoenician) is one of the most important alphabets among what are wrongly called Semitic languages[18]. These researchers believe that it is the origin of other alphabets such as Greek, Syriac, Arabic, Hebrew, Mandaic, and... It is the mother of all the pens of the world, whether directly or indirectly.

Thanks to its alphabet and the ease of derivation in its language, the Aramaic language was able to spread rapidly, especially in Mesopotamia, Canaan, and Persia. It gradually replaced the Akkadian (Babylonian-Assyrian) language in the East, where it was adopted as a common language of communication in the Neo-

---

[18] Bishop Andrew Sanna (Council Magazine No. 1.2 - Between Arabic and Syriac) Father Albert Abuna (Aramaic Language Literature) Ahmed Sousse (Arabs and Jews in History)

Assyrian Empire by Tiglath-Pileser III during the eighth century. BC, and was preserved by the peoples of the Neo-Babylonian (Chaldean) Empire and the Achaemenid Empire.

In the year 539 BC, when the Achaemenids, led by Cyrus the Persian, occupied Babylon, Aramaic was spoken and written from the borders of Iran to Egypt[19], and Darius (521-485) gave it a new impetus by using the form (Imperial Aramaic) as one of the official languages of the Persian Empire. When he installed a cuneiform inscription in ancient Persian, Elamite, and Babylonian on the face of the Beistun Rock, he prepared Aramaic translations of the text that were sent to distant fields such as southern Egypt, and Aramaic inscriptions were also discovered From this era in far eastern regions such as Afghanistan.

The Aramaic language remained the auxiliary language for the entire region from Egypt to Iran until the conquests of Alexander in the late fourth century BC; When Greek began to replace it in some places. Likewise, the Canaanite languages, including Hebrew, were replaced in the West, and some books of the Torah were written in them[20].

Thanks to the expansion of these empires (Assyrian, Chaldean, Persian/Achaemenid), the spread of Aramaic

---

The Aramaic language and ancient libraries / Harry Sacks - Translated by: [19]
Saeed Al-Ghanimi
https://annabaa.org/arabic/arts/5876
[20] Dr.. Khaled Hussein / Journal of the Syriac Language Academy - No. 8 of 1984, p. 51 Dr.. Khaled Hussein / Journal of the Syriac Language Academy - No. 8 of 1984, p. 51

expanded to dominate the entire East, becoming the language of correspondence between the governments and peoples of the region. The Old Testament indicates that the ministers of King Hezekiah (Eliqaym, Shebna, and Joah) asked Rabshaga[21], the commander of the forces of the Assyrian Emperor Sennacherib ( 705-681 BC) to address them in Aramaic (Speak to your servants in Aramaic, for we understand it)

The language of trade and administration was not Akkadian, but Aramaic[22], as the Aramaic alphabet replaced the cuneiform writing due to its ease. Plates written in Akkadian or Pahlavi often carried translations of them in Aramaic for the benefit of merchants.

It became the language of circulation and writing between the Assyrian and Persian empires and the states within its orbit. The educated class took it as a tool for writing and expression, especially during the era of Sennacherib and afterward, due to its ease. Dr. Adnan Hamid Taha Elwes[23] says in his thesis submitted to the University of Wales: The description of the Aramaic script as the Assyrian script is clear evidence of the extensive use of Aramaic in the Assyrian Empire.

---

[21] 36:11    Isaiah 36:11
[22] D. George Rahma and Mitri Wahba / Aramaic - Syriac language and heritage.
[23] The use of Aramaic in the Neo-Assyrian Empire - Dr. Khaled Ismail/ Journal of the Iraqi Scientific Academy - Syriac Language Authority - Volume 9, 1985, p. 291

Some Assyrian kings used Aramaic scribes, and it was the official language of the Babylonian court until the end of the Persian era.

This appears clearly in the Wisdom of Ahikar (the scribe of the Assyrian king Sennacherib and Esarhaddon and bearer of his seals), dating back to the seventh century BC. It was found on the island of Umm al-Fila - Upper Egypt, written on papyrus.

A letter was also found in Egypt, written in Aramaic on papyrus, sent by King Adon, the prince of one of the Phoenician cities, to the king of Egypt in about the year 605 BC, asking him to support him in repelling the Chaldean-Babylonian armies[24].

There are also letters exchanged between the Persian Emperor and one of his agents in Egypt, published by Driver[25] in Aramaic Documents. They consist of ten letters written on leather (possibly parchment) and found in a leather wallet. They originate in Babylon and Shushan. It is addressed to the employee of the Persian Emperor in Egypt. It is Persian with its Aramaic script and was discovered after the discovery of the papyrus leaves (The Book of the Wisdom of Ahiqar). All of them date back to the beginning of the fifth century BC (490 - 408 BC) and extend to about the year 300 BC.

---

[24] DuPont Sommer / Sommer magazine, issue 19, 1963, translated by Father Albert Abouna, p. 137

[25] Bishop Boulos Behnam - New Horizons in the Study of the Aramaic Language / Journal of the Syriac Language Academy - Volume 2, 1976, p. 347

These letters and documents exchanged between these countries were in the Aramaic language, which was the language of writing and literature in Assyria since the seventh century BC. They appeared written in ink on seals and records, contrary to what was used by the Assyrians (engraving on stone tablets).

In addition to the Behistun platform, which dates back to the sixth century BC, it was found on Mount Behistun (Persia) in Kermanshah Province in Iran. The inscription includes three versions of the same text, written in three different languages (Babylonian Cuneiform, Elamite Persian, and Aramaic), and was crucial in deciphering the cuneiform texts.

The inscription was authenticated by Darius I, sometime between his coronations as king of the Persian Empire in 522 BC.

There are many evidences found in Afghanistan, India, Persia, Babylon, Assyria, Palestine, the Arabian Peninsula, Egypt, and... Written in Aramaic script, some in Karshuni and others in Aramaic…

Father Lammens the Jesuit believes that Aramaic has even surpassed Greek in spread, so he says[26]:

(One of the strangest things is that the spread of the Syriac-Aramaic language reached a great extent during the reign of the Seleucids, and it became the dominant Syriac language in Syria, Mesopotamia, Iraq, the Arabian Peninsula, and Armenia. This language extended to

---

[26] Bishop George Havory, p. 20, quoted from Al-Sharq Magazine, p. 705-

China, India, and the Nile. We do not think that any other language, not even Greek, has rivaled Syriac in its breadth, with the exception of English at present).

Aramaic ascended its golden throne from the time of the Chaldean Empire, then Persian (Achaemenid) until the middle of the fourth century BC, when its star began to decline after Alexander the Great took control of the countries of the East, so Greek became the official language in the region, which led Aramaic to branch into scripts and dialects, and little by little these dialects moved away from each other. Especially after the death of Alexander and the division of his kingdom in 323 BC into states Communication between the Aramaic people was cut off, and as a result of their mixing with other peoples, and being influenced by their languages, each according to their location, several dialects and scripts arose for us today, including the Palestinian dialect, the Nabataean dialect, the Palmyra dialect, the Rahavian dialect, the Babylonian (Talmud of Babylon), and the Mandaean dialect, some of which disappeared, and others remained, such as the Syriac, Mandaic, Hebrew, and Arabic script.

The ancient Aramaic alphabet was used to write the languages spoken by ancient pre-Christian tribes throughout the Fertile Crescent. It was then adopted by other groups as an easy alphabet, such as the Assyrians and Chaldeans, who permanently replaced the letters of their cuneiform language with Aramaic, and the Achaemenid Persians and Jews, who adopted Aramaic as their vernacular language. They began to use the Aramaic alphabet even to write the Hebrew language, displacing the previous ancient Hebrew alphabet with the exception of the modern Samaritan alphabet, which was derived from ancient Hebrew.

The Aramaic script became used in writing the Torah, the Talmud, and in classical Jewish literature, and the name given to Modern Hebrew writing was "Ashurit"[27].

The bottom line:

The first known Aramaic inscriptions, date back to the late 10th or early 9th century BC. In a massive wave of expansion, the Aramaic alphabet and its language spread throughout Palestine, Syria, Iraq, Iran, Egypt, Saudi Arabia, and large areas of Asia, replacing many languages, including Akkadian, Hebrew, and…For nearly a thousand years it served as the official written language of the Near East. The expansion of the Aramaic script, first by the Assyrians and then by the Chaldean and Achaemenid Empire, helped the spread of the Aramaic script, which adopted Aramaic as its official language, replacing the Akkadian language.

During the subsequent Chaldean (Neo-Babylonian) and Persian conquests, Aramaic became the international medium of exchange despite the Hellenistic influences that followed the conquests of Alexander the Great of

---

[27] It is believed that during the period of Assyrian domination, the Aramaic writing and language acquired official status
It is believed that during the period of Assyrian domination, Aramaic writing and language gained official status
seehttps://ar.wikipedia.org/wiki/%D8%A7%
https://www.pathsofjordan.net/the-rock-art/some-notions-about-the-pre-islamic-inscriptions-of-the-jordanian-deserts-and-beyond

Macedon, Especially in the cities where Aramaic remained the vernacular language of the defeated peoples in the Holy Lands, Syria, Mesopotamia, and neighboring countries. This writing and language in its new form (Syriac) did not destabilize until the ninth century AD, that is, two full centuries after the Islamic conquest of Damascus in 633 and Jerusalem in 635. However, the Arabic language never completely replaced Aramaic.

Aramaic was adopted by the exiled Jews of Transjordan (exiles from Bashan and Gilead) in 732 BC. Led by Tiglath-Pileser III. And the tribes of the northern kingdom led by Sargon II, who captured Samaria in 721, and the tribes of the southern kingdom of Judah, who were captured by Nebuchadnezzar to Babylon in 587. So when the Jews returned from Babylonian captivity, they took Aramaic with them, and this remained their mother tongue for a long time.

## The alphabets that emerged from Aramaic

| Arabic | Hebrew | Mandaean | Syriac | | Hatra | Palmyra | Nabatieh | Ancient Aramaic |
|--------|--------|----------|--------|--|-------|---------|----------|-----------------|
| ا | א | | ܐ | | | | | |
| ب | ב | | ܒ | | | | | |
| ج | ג | | | | | | | |

| | | | | | | | |
|---|---|---|---|---|---|---|---|
| د | ד | | | | | | |
| ه | ה | | | | | | |
| و | ו | | | | | | |
| ز | ז | | | | | | |
| ح | ח | | | | | | |
| ط | ט | | | | | | |
| ي | ׳ | | | | | | |
| ك | כ — ך | | | | | | |
| ل | ל | | | | | | |
| م | מ — ם | | | | | | |
| ن | נ — ן | | | | | | |
| س | ס | | | | | | |
| ع | ע | | | | | | |
| ف | פ — ף | | | | | | |
| ص | צ — ץ | | | | | | |
| ق | ק | | | | | | |

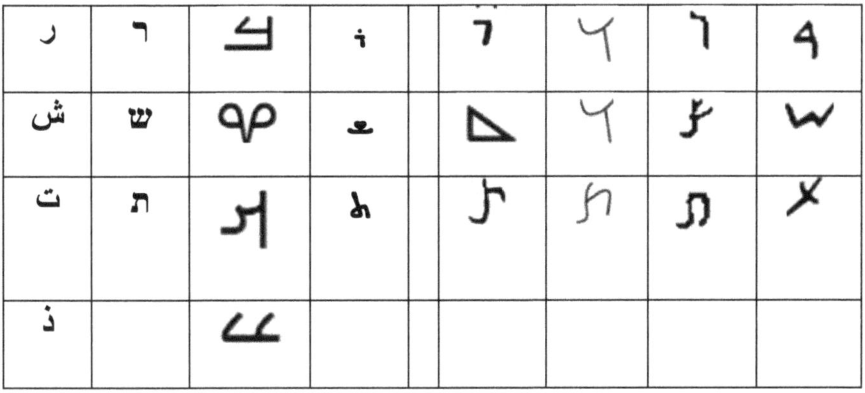

| | | | | | | | |
|---|---|---|---|---|---|---|---|
| ر | ٦ | ⊐ | ٠ | ٦ | Υ | ٦ | ⊄ |
| ش | ש | φ | ٠ | ◁ | Υ | ʓ | W |
| ت | ת | ⊣ | ٨ | ٢ | ʃʋ | ⅅ | Х |
| ذ | | ∠∠ | | | | | |

If we look closely at the drawing of the letters, we will see the:

1- The lettering (Syriac, Hebrew, Arabic) is derived from the drawing of the imperial Aramaic letters or from Nabataean, Palmyra, and Hatrian.

2- As for Mandaic, we will find most of its letters similar to Syriac, Arabic, Hebrew, and Aramaic, but not from the letter that corresponds to its letters. Rather, in many cases we find the drawing of the letter similar to the drawing of another letter.

It is worth mentioning:

The Mandaeans in Iraq and Iran still use Aramaic writing. In comparison with ancient manuscripts from the regions where the Mandaeans were present, Some argue that the Mandaic script[28] is a product of the late Parthian

---

[28] Iranian texts of the Aramaic languages: origin of the Mandaic script
Charles J. Hexperl / Department of Near Eastern Languages and Civilizations / Harvard University

period (more specifically the 2nd century AD) and has close associations with a range of scripts ranging from Anatolia and the Caucasus in the north to Elemis in the south, all of which appear to have been derived from or strongly influenced by the Parthian script. The association of the Mandaeans with the later Arsacids also reflects this through their myths and textual traditions others argue that the Mandaic script is derived from the Palmyra script or from the Nabataean script, like other cursive scripts such as Syriac or Arabic. Perhaps this means that the Mandaean script must have originated in Syria and moved west with the Mandaeans, and this view was adopted by (Leadzbarsky 1909; Rudolf Makuch 1971).

Others (Joseph Naveh 1970) on it (the Mandaic script) being derived from the Elymian language - the script attested on later coins of Elymis (modern Khuzestan in Iran) in the 2nd century AD, when Elymis was a kingdom of the Parthian Empire.

# Second: The emergenceof Sabaean and Jiziya alphabets

Researchers believe that the Sabaean writing in the south of the Arabian Peninsula and Abyssinia dates back to the eighth century BC, and perhaps a little earlier, in light of the inscriptions discovered, which were called the Sabaean script (Musnad). Evidence of it was found in the form of inscriptions has been found in Yemen, Saudi Arabia, Eritrea, Ethiopia, and Somalia dating back to the first millennium BC. Other inscriptions were also found at the site of Qasr al-Banat on the Egyptian Qena Road, as well as in Giza, and Dr. Jawad Ali's beliefs date back to the third century BC.

It seems that writing in the Musnad script remained in circulation, especially in Yemen, until a period close to Islam, that is, until the sixth century AD, such as southern Arabic writings, such as the inscription called (Hisn Ghurab)[29], which commemorates the victory of the Abyssinians over the Yemenis in the year 524 AD.

Another text was written by Abraha, the ruler of Yemen during the reign of the Abyssinians, ordered to be written and placed on the walls of the Ma'rib Dam when he restored and repaired the dam in the year 542 AD. The most recent text found dates back to the year 554 AD, according to the Iraqi historian Dr. Jawad Ali.

---

[29] D. Jawad Ali / Al-Mufassal fi History of the Arabs Before Islam, Part 1, 1993, 2nd Edition, p. 44

Third: The emergence of the Gee'z alphabet:

The Geéz writing system is one of the oldest working systems in the world. This writing system has remained in circulation in the region unchanged for 2,000 years, due to its ability to adapt and its innovative way of organizing sounds[30].

Geez: It is the language previously used in Ethiopia and Eritrea, and it became the official language of the Kingdom of Axum and the Ethiopian Imperial Palace.

The Geez language and its script, as some sources say, descend from the Himyarite language that was used in southern Arabia, meaning Yemen, in the seventh century BC, and it is derived from the Sabaean language.

The Himyarites who migrated to Abyssinia (according to some studies) before Christ carried this script with them, so the Geez language took it as a means of writing, and then the

Abyssinians developed it, so they deleted from it the letters

(tha', dha', dha', ghān, and sāmekh )

(الثاء ، الذال والظاء والغين والسامخ ).

Because these sounds do not exist in their language and they added signs for the vowels to it. By affixation method, each letter has seven forms.

---

[30] Evidence of Writing Systems from the Antiquity of Eritrea
By Abraham Zerai | Eritrea Profile

Then Amharic, which became the state language of Abyssinia in the 13th century AD, took it and added letters to it for sounds unknown in Sabaean and made some modifications to it. However, some believe the opposite, that is, the language was transferred from Ethiopia and Eritrea to the Arabian Peninsula.

It is generally agreed that the Gezi writing system had achieved perfection by the 4th or 5th century AD when Geezah was preserved, in practice, across a wide range of sacred and scholarly activities from the 13th to the 17th centuries AD, known as the "Classical Period" of Gezi literature.

The Sabaean and Geez languages have no relation to the Arabic language in which the Qur'an and Mu'allaqat in general were written, and this is what I noticed in the inscriptions discovered in Saudi Arabia, Yemen, Ethiopia, Eritrea, and Somalia. This is what Al-Qurtubi reached in his introduction to the interpretation, and Taha Hussein went on to explain the wide difference between the Arabic languages and the ancient languages which be used in southern Arabia during the seventh century BC.

The Geez language, like the Sabaean language, has separate letters and is written from right to left, and sometimes vice versa (from left to right).

The mother tongue, Geez, is used today only in the Ethiopian and Eritrean Churches, and it is also used by Ethiopian Jewish communities. Two major languages emerged from it: Amharic and Tigrinya:

1-The Tigrinya language: It is the national and official language of the State of Eritrea, as it is a spoken and read language, unlike other local languages. It is considered one of the languages spread in East Africa, and the number of its speakers is more than 7 million people, divided between Eritrea and Ethiopia.

The Arabic script was used to write the Tigri language officially during the Ottoman and Egyptian Khedive rule.

The Amharic language: It is the official language of Ethiopia, spoken by the inhabitants of Ethiopia, and it is the second most widespread of the so-called Semitic languages, after Arabic.

A small number of inscriptions were found in both Eritrea and Ethiopia, most of which are written in Musnad script, and their scholars have assumed that their first archaeological inscriptions were written in the seventh century or even in the eighth century BC.

However, what was discovered does not match their civilizations compared to what was found in Yemen and Saudi Arabia, and the reason, I believe, is the economic poverty of the two countries. Therefore, these two countries were not able to attract excavation missions to excavate there, and I am confident that there are thousands of inscriptions still buried. There are inscriptions written in Aramaic script among them.

The Geez language disappeared as a living language around the year 1000 AD, but it remained the language of religious rituals in the Ethiopian and Eritrean Church and was replaced by Tigrinya and Amharic.

# The relationship of the Geez line to the Musnad line

Many sources say that the writing in the inscriptions discovered in the region (Ethiopia, Eritrea, and Somalia) has its roots in Yemen, meaning that the Yemenis who migrated to the region (Ethiopia, Eritrea, and Somalia) carried the Sabaean Himyarite script with them. In my opinion, the reason lies perhaps because excavations took place in Yemen before Eritrea, Ethiopia, and Somalia, so at first they thought that writing moved from Yemen to there.

This was rejected by the linguists James Theodore Bent, David Heinrich Müller, and John George Garson in the nineteenth century. They went on to say that the ancient Ethiopian-Eritrean inscription in (Yha) is older than any other inscription found in the Arabian Peninsula (Saudi Arabia and Yemen). There are even slight differences.

Likewise, there is no indication in the sources of the southern Arabian Peninsula of any migration, whatever its form, from this country to Ethiopia, Eritrea, or Somalia at that time[31]. This means that we have to reconsider the theory that the writing in Ethiopia and

---

[31] Reconsidering contacts between southern Arabia and the highlands of Tigrai in the 1st millennium BC
Fabienne Dugast & Iwona Gajda UMR "Orient & Méditerranée", Paris
https://shs.hal.science/halshs-00865945/document

Eritrea was transmitted by some residents of Yemen who immigrated to the region.

Other scholars argue that the Arabian Peninsula was first colonized by the Ethiopians, and not the other way around, as documented in ancient literature[32] (see the History of Ethiopia/Kush page).

If an invasion or occupation occurred during the time of the Kingdom of Demet, then there is no doubt that writing was transferred from Ethiopia or Eritrea to the Arabian Peninsula. However, if the occupation occurred during the time of the Aksumite Kingdom, that is, in the first or second century BC, and perhaps after AD, then this is a question mark because the inscriptions were written down before that.

In other words, "Old Ethiopic Eritrea" is older and somewhat different from the Sabaean script which is a syllabic script similar to Ge'ez. Whereas the word "Sabain" itself is derived from the Geezian word (Saba), which modern Ethiopians call (Makeda), who is the leader of (Damt).

In addition to the presence of ancient inscriptions discovered in Ethiopia and Eritrea written in the Sabaean and Geez scripts, the Geez language (with its Amharic and Tigrinya branches) is still spoken in the region. At the time, the Sabaean language disappeared from Yemen and Saudi Arabia.

---

[32] Ancient Inscription Blocks from Yeha, Ethiopia, Africa
Oldest script south of the Sahara at Yeha
http://solarey.net/ancient-inscription-blocks-from-yeha-ethiopia-africa

All of this makes me lean toward the theory of language transmission from the region (Ethiopia and Eritrea) to the Arabian Peninsula and not the other way around.

Therefore, we have to re-evaluate and discuss the nature of contacts between the Tigray highlands and southern Arabia in the first millennium BC, as well as the chronology of this period.

Ethiopian and Eritrean inscriptions and buildings look very similar to those found in southern Arabia according to excavations.

On the other hand, some argue that the written data constitute an important body of evidence regarding the Yemeni relationship or presence, The alphabet, the written form, and even the language and its main features clearly indicate the existence of similar texts on both sides of the Red Sea (the first millennium BC and AD), and they called the writing in it the Sabaic script.

Since the script appeared at a close time in the southern Arabian Peninsula and in Ethiopia and Eritrea, according to the findings of researcher Jacqueline Perenne[33] [Pirenne 1956] by comparing the style of the paleographic inscriptions on both sides. In its early stage - type A and B according to its classification, whereas the first archaeological inscriptions were either contemporary or the South Arabian inscriptions may have occurred slightly earlier (a few decades) under Jacqueline's classification. Therefore, it can be assumed

---

[33] Reconsidering contacts between southern Arabia And the highlands of Tigraiinthe  BC according  toepigraphic  data Fabienne  Dugast,Iwona Gajda

today (and this is by Jacqueline Perrin) that the first archaeological inscriptions were written in Ethiopia/Eritrea in the seventh century or even the eighth century BC.

The ancient hypothesis according to which the script appeared in Ethiopia and Eritrea in the 5th century BC, and based on comparison with the chronology of ancient southern Arabia previously proposed (The chronology was recently confirmed through radiocarbon analysis of the first construction phase of the Almaqa Temple in the Gawa cemetery, located in northern Ethiopia near Axum - the oldest archaeological buildings in that country). As the scientists Nootnick and Wolf say [Wolf & Nowotnick 2010. This is what is now rejected by both the scholars De Maigret and Robin [De Maigret & Robin 1998]. Studies related to these inscriptions by their discoverers indicate that the text often represents a supplication to a god. This is what is now rejected by both the scholars De Maigret and Robin [De Maigret & Robin 1998][34].

 Studies related to these inscriptions by their discoverers indicate that the text often represents a supplication to a god. But it is roughly engraved on rocks or stones it can be described as graffiti; Most of them content themselves with giving a personal name linked to religious symbols, especially in the Senafi region (Eritrea).

It must be noted that the style of writing in the plowing method (plowing the land) in the Ethiopian and Somali

---

[34] Reconsidering contacts between southern Arabia And the highlands of Tigraiinthe BC according toepigraphic data Fabienne Dugast,Iwona Gajda https://shs.hal.science/halshs-00865945/document

Eritrean inscriptions is not found in the Sabaean inscriptions discovered in Saudi Arabia and Yemen, nor in the Aramaic inscriptions.

That is, the first line is read from right to left, but in the second line, you find writing in the opposite direction, based on the direction the letter is drawn.

This means that the first line starts from right to left (or vice versa), in the second line from left to right, in the third from right to left, in the fourth from left to right, and so on in the rest of the lines, as if the copyist was passing his hand continuously, that is, he starts from the right side Which ended without returning to the first side. That is, it starts from the place where it ended without returning to the first place. This may be a result of Greek or Roman influence, who wrote from left to right.

Given the similarity of this style of writing between Ethiopian, Eritrean, and Somali, and its difference from what is found in Yemeni writing, this is evidence that the writing moved from Ethiopian, Eritrean, and Somali to Somalia, and not from Yemen.

The Geez alphabet consists of 26 letters, including a symbol

).⟍ (p) and a kamal (g

While the Sabaean is 29 letters devoid of these two letters. 26 letters, most of which are similar to the Sabaean letters, except for the letters:

| | Aramaic | Sabaean | Geez | Arabic |
|---|---|---|---|---|

| | | | |
|---|---|---|---|
| | ꟼ | Ϥ | д |
| But it resembles the Aramaic letter ⊟ H' or dha in the Musnad Ⱨ DH | Ȣ | H | ز |
| ⊕ | ⴰ | ⵔ | ط |
| ι | 1 | Λ | ل |
| 7 | ◊ | Ȣ | ف |
| φ | ộ | ф | ق |
| W | ⌇ | Ш | ش |

In addition to the presence of the letters (TH, DH, samekh, Z', GH) in the Sabaean and their absence in the Geez, there is a similarity between Ugaritic, Sabaean, Geez, and after them Arabic, in the use of some letters

(kh, dh, dha, th, jg / ‫خ، ذ، ظ، ث، غ‬ )

The letter (Ḍād) is found in Sabaean, but is absent in Ugaritic.

The letters (‫ئ، و‬) are found in Ugaritic, but they are absent in Sabaean and Geez.

> 3- Phoenician and Aramaic are devoid of these letters despite the proximity of their locations.

(Kh, dh, dha, tha, gh, dha ؤ،ئ)

(خ ، ذ ، ظ ، ث ، غ ، ض ، ئ، ؤ )

In contrast, the owners of the Sabaean and Geez alphabets are far from the birthplaces of Ugaritic.

# The alphabet

| Arabic | Sabaean | Geezy | Hebrew | Syriac | Aramaic |
|---|---|---|---|---|---|
| ا | ħ | አ | א | ܐ | ✝ |
| ب | Ⴖ | ∩ | ב | ܒ | ₰ |
| ج | ٦ | ٦ | ג | ܓ | ٦ |
| د | ۷ | ₽ | ד | ܕ | ۹ |
| ه | Ψ | U | ה | ܗ | ∃ |
| و | Φ | ⊞ | ו | ܘ | Ч |
| ز | ୪ | Η | ז | ܙ | I |
| ح | Ψ | ⊹ | ח | ܚ | ⊞ |
| ط | 0 | ⋔ | ט | ܛ | ⊕ |
| ي | ९ | የ | י | ܝ | Ⴧ |
| ك | ∩ | ħ | כ – ך | ܟ | ٦ |
| ل | 1 | ۸ | ל | ܠ | ل |
| م | ৪ | ⊞ | ם – מ | ܡ | ⅍ |
| ن | Ⴗ | ٦ | ן | ܢ | ⅁ |
| س | ∧ | ∩ | ס | ܣ | ‡ |

| Arabic | Sabaean | Geezy | Hebrew | Syriac | Aramaic |
|--------|---------|-------|--------|--------|---------|
| ع | O | 0 | ע | ـ | O |
| Arabic | Sabaean | Geezy | Hebrew | Syriac | Aramaic |
| ف | | | פ – ף | | |
| ص | | | צ – ץ | | |
| ق | | | ק | | |
| ر | | | ר | | |
| ش | | | ש | | |
| ت | | | ת | | |
| خ | | | | | |
| ض | | | | | |
| ث | | | | | |
| ث | | | | | |
| ذ | | | | | |
| سامخ | | | | | |

| ظ | ሸ | | | | |
|---|---|---|---|---|---|
| غ | ሰ | | 48 | | |

# Chapter 4

# Derivation of the letters of the common alphabets

**1-** Is Ugaritic considered the basis of the region's alphabet?

Certainly, one of us will wonder, what is the origin of these alphabets (Phoenician, Aramaic, Sabaean, and Geezian)? Can we say that Ugaritic, with its cuneiform symbols, is the

?original

If we look closely at these alphabets, we will see:

1-Ugaritic has a small number of symbols, namely:

( ‹ , ⊣< , ▷⊢ , ⊢— )

But it made 30 letters out of it, through repetition or change of direction.

2-There is a similarity between Ugaritic, Sabaean, Geezian, and after them Arabic, using some letters like

خ ، ذ ، ظ ، ث ، غ (kh, dh, dha, th, g - in Sabaea, but ض)And the presence of the letter (dha

its absence in Ugaritic.

in Ugaritic and its (ؤ ، ئ) The presence of letters absence in Sabaean.

3- Phoenician and Aramaic are devoid of these letters despite the proximity of their locations.

((Kh, dh, dha, tha, gh, dha, ey, d ḍ)

( ؤ ،ئ ، ض ، غ ، ث ، ظ ، ذ ، خ)

In contrast, the owners of the Sabaean and Geez alphabets are far from the birthplaces of Ugaritic.

4- There is a great similarity between Phoenician and Aramaic, which made scholars believe that Phoenician is the basis of Aramaic, and so it is between the Sabaean and the Geezian, which led scholars to say that the Sabaean is the origin of the Geezian, and others the opposite.

5- There is some similarity in the drawing basis of some Ugaritic letters with Phoenician, Aramaic, Sabaean, and Geezian, for example:

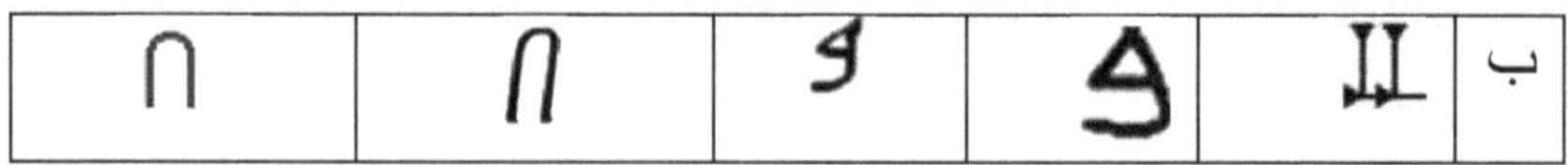

**And:**

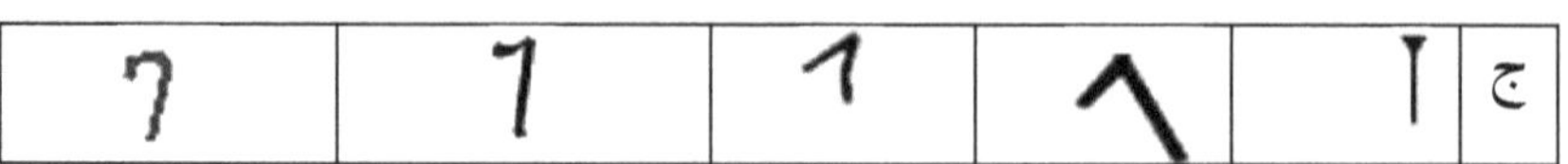

**And:**

| ∩ | ∧ | ‡ | ≢ | ⋮⋮ | ش |
|---|---|---|---|---|---|

And other…

| B | Ⅱ | ◁ | ৭ | ∩ | ∩ |
|---|---|---|---|---|---|
| G | Ⅰ | ∧ | ৴ | ˥ | ? |
| S | ⋮⋮ | ≢ | ‡ | ∧ | ∩ |

# 2– Derivation of the alphabets used:

First group (Abjad)

| Arabic | Mandaic | Hebrew | Syriac | Gees | Palmyra | Hatra | Nabataean | Sabaean | Imperial Aramaic | Phoenician | Canaanite |
|---|---|---|---|---|---|---|---|---|---|---|---|
| ا | ○ | א | ܐ | አ | ✕ | ⊔ | ⊻ | ħ | ✝ | ✖ | ⊢ |
| ب | ⊥ | ב | ܒ | ∩ | У | ⊔ | ⊃ | ∩ | ৭ | ◁ | Ⅱ |
| ج | ৪ | ג | ✓ | ৲ | ⅄ | ⊥ | ⅄ | ˥ | ৴ | ∧ | Ⅰ |
| د | ⊔ | ד | ◌ | ₽ | ⅄ | ٦ | ٦ | ┩ | ◀ | △ | Ⅲ |

Where did these letters come from?

| Letter | Mandaic | Arabic | Hebrew | Syriac | Gees |
|---|---|---|---|---|---|
| A | It looks like (w) in Syriac | It looks like Western Syriac | It looks like Palmyra | It looks like Nabataean, Hatra | It looks like Sabaean |
| B | It looks like (sh) in Syriac | It looks like Nabataean | It looks like Nabataean | It looks like Nabataean | It looks like Sabaean |
| J | It looks like (a) in Syriac but opposite direction | It looks like a little Nabataean, Hatra | It looks like Palmyra | It looks like Nabataean, Hatra | It looks like Sabaean, Phoenician |
| D | It looks like (b, w) in Imperial Aramaic | It looks like Nabataean, Hatra | It looks like Nabataean, Hatra | It looks like Nabataean, Hatra | Imperial Aramaic |

## Second group (hwz)

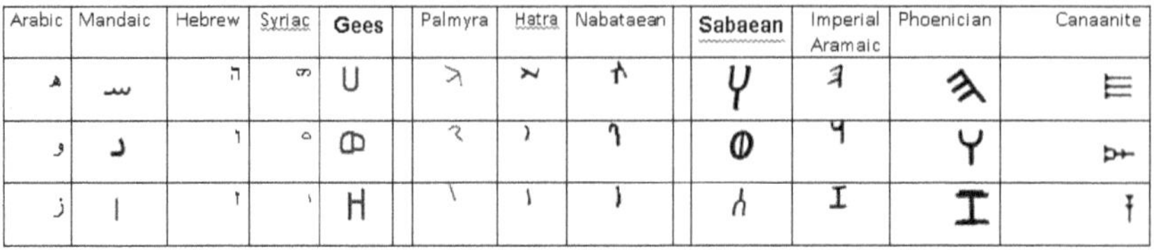

| Arabic | Mandaic | Hebrew | Syriac | Gees | Palmyra | Hatra | Nabataean | Sabaean | Imperial Aramaic | Phoenician | Canaanite |
|---|---|---|---|---|---|---|---|---|---|---|---|
| ه | � | ה | ܗ | U | ⋋ | ⋋ | ↑ | Ψ | ⅂ | ⋛ | ☰ |
| و | ﻟ | ו | ܘ | ⵙ | ⌒ | ) | ⌐ | Φ | ⵑ | Υ | ⵑ |
| ز | ﺍ | ז | ، | H | ⟍ | ） | ） | ⅄ | I | I | ⵑ |

### Where did these letters come from?

| Letter | Mandaean | Arabic | Hebrew | Syriac | Gees |
|---|---|---|---|---|---|
| H | It looks like ( ﺳ H') Syriac and (s) Arabic | It looks like a bit like Syriac | It looks like the Nabataean letter T | Independent | It looks like a bit Sabaean |
| W | It looks like (d) Syriac, Arabic | It looks like Nabataean | It looks like a bit Nabataean, Palmyra and Hatra | It looks like the letter A' ʿAramaic | It looks like Sabaean |
| Z | It looks like (z) Imperial Aramaic | It looks like Nabataean, Syriac | It looks like to the Phoenician and Aramaic | It looks like Hatra | It looks like a bit letter H' ﺡ in Aramaic |

## Third group (hty)

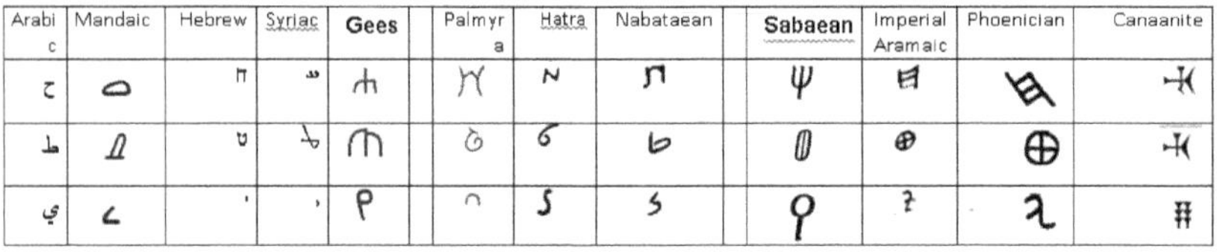

| Arabic | Mandaic | Hebrew | Syriac | Gees | Palmyra | Hatra | Nabataean | Sabaean | Imperial Aramaic | Phoenician | Canaanite |
|---|---|---|---|---|---|---|---|---|---|---|---|
| ح | ◠ | ח | ﺤ | ⼐ | ⴶ | N | ⊓ | Ψ | ⊟ | ⬧ | ⵑ |
| ط | ⌁ | ט | ⌐ | ⋒ | ⊙ | ʹ | ⅃ | ⎘ | ⊕ | ⊕ | ⵑ |
| ع | ⌐ | ، | ، | ⵔ | ⌒ | ⌁ | ⌁ | ⵔ | ? | ⵌ | ⌗ |

### Where did these letters come from?

| Letter | Mandaean | Arabic | Hebrew | Syriac | Gees |
|---|---|---|---|---|---|
| ﺡ H' | It looks like a bit (w) in Syriac | Independent | It looks like Nabataean | Independent | It looks like Sabaean upside down |
| T | Independent | It looks like Syriac | It looks like Palmyra | It looks like a bit like Nabataean | It looks like a bit Sabaean |
| Y | It looks like a (L) in Hatra | It looks like Syriac After putting two dots under the letter | It looks like Palmyra, Syriac | It looks like a Palmyra upside down | It looks like Sabaean |

## Forth group (KLMN)

| Arabic | Mandaic | Hebrew | Syriac | Gees | Palmyra | Hatra | Nabataean | Sabaean | Imperial Aramaic | Phoenician | Canaanite |
|---|---|---|---|---|---|---|---|---|---|---|---|
| ك | ᗐ | כ - ך | ᐣ | h | ᗄ | ] | כ | 𝑓 | ᐟ | ⅄ | ⊢ |
| ل | ⅃ | ל | ᒐ | ᐱ | ⅂ | ⅃ | ς | 1 | ι | ᐸ | Ⅲ |
| م | ᔑ | מ - ם | ᵱ | ⊓ⅅ | ᗑ | ᚴ | מ | 𝔙 | ᓬ | ᵱ | ⊣ |
| ن | V | נ | ᔈ | ᒕ | ᒕ | J | ⅃ | 𝟒 | ᓬ | ᑦ | ⟼ |

### Where did these letters come from?

| Letter | Mandaean | Arabic | Hebrew | Syriac | Gees |
|---|---|---|---|---|---|
| K | It looks like a bit (n) in Aramaic | Independent | It looks like Nabatean and Hatra | It looks like a bit Palmyra | It looks like Sabaean |
| L | It looks a Syriac | It looks like Syriac and Hatra | It looks like Palmyra and Hatra | It looks like Hatra | Independent |
| M | Independent | It looks like Western م Syriac | It looks like Nabataean, Palmyra and Hatra | It looks like Nabataean , Palmyra and Hatra | It looks like Sabaean in the opposite direction |
| N | Independent | It looks like Syriac after putting dot on the letter | It looks like Syriac | It looks like Nabataean and Hatra | It looks like Sabaean |

## Fifth group (safs ص ف ع س)

| Arabic | Mandaic | Hebrew | Syriac | Gees | Palmyra | Hatra | Nabataean | Sabaean | Imperial Aramaic | Phoenician | Canaanite |
|---|---|---|---|---|---|---|---|---|---|---|---|
| س | ᔑ | ס | ∞ | ⋔ | ᑦ | ᖙ | ᵱ | 𝝬ᖆ | ᚶ | ᚶ | ⫲ Ⴑ |
| ع | ᔍ | ע | ᒪ | 0 | ⋎ | ⟩ | ᵧ | O | ° | O | ⟨ |
| ف | ᗷ | פ - ף | ᵱ | ᗡ ᒑ | ᗡ | ꝗ | ᒒ | ᗝ | ᒉ | ᒉ | ⊨ |
| ص | ᗞ | צ - ץ | ᵴ | ᗞ | ᐢ | ᒕ | ᒑ | ᗮ | ᒉ | ᔐ | Ⅱ |

### Where did these letters come from?

| Letter | Mandaean | Arabic | Hebrew | Syriac | Geziah |
|---|---|---|---|---|---|
| س | It looks like ( S' ص) In Arabic | Independent | It looks like Phoenician and Aramaic | It looks like a bit Nabataean | It looks like Sabaean |
| ع | It looks like (k) in Arabic | It looks like Palmyra and Nabataean | It looks like Palmyra and Nabataean | It looks like Palmyra and Nabataean | It looks like Sabaean, Phoenician, and Aramaic |
| ف | It looks like (f) in Arabic Without a point | It looks like Syriac and Hatra | It looks like Hatra | It looks like Hatra | independent |
| ص | It looks like (s) in Arabic | It looks like Hatra | It looks like Hatra | It looks like Hatra | It looks like Sabaean |

sixth group (Qrshat)

| Arabic | Mandaic | Hebrew | Syriac | Gees | Palmyra | Hatra | Nabataean | Sabaean | Imperial Aramaic | Phoenician | Canaanite |
|---|---|---|---|---|---|---|---|---|---|---|---|
| ق | ⊬ | ק | ܩ | Ⴔ | ܝܕ | ܚ | ܝ | Ⴍ | Ⴔ | Ⴔ | ⊢ |
| ر | ⊿ | ר | ܝ | ∠ | ۷ | ۲ | ٦ | ۶ | ۹ | ۹ | ⊬ |
| ش | ۹۹ | שׁ | ܫ | Ш | ۷ | ◿ | ۶ | ۶ | w | W | ⟨V⟩ |
| ت | Ⴈ | ת | ܬ | ✝ | ۾ | ✔ | ♫ | χ | ✗ | ✚ | — |

Where did these letters come from?

| Letter | Mandaean | Arabic | Hebrew | Syriac | Geziah |
|---|---|---|---|---|---|
| Q | It looks like (m) in Syriac | It looks like Syriac Just put two dots above the letter | independent | independent | It looks like Phoenician, Aramaic And Sabaean |
| R | It looks like (b, w) in Imperial Aramaic | It looks like Sabaean and Hatra | It looks like Nabataean and Hatra | It looks like Nabataean and Hatra | It looks like a bit Sabaean opposite direction |
| SH | independent | It looks like a bit Phoenician and Aramaic | It looks like a bit Phoenician and Aramaic | It looks like a bit Aramaic | It looks like Phoenician, Aramaic And abet Sabaean |
| T | It looks like a bit (m) in Aramaic | independent | independent | It looks like Palmyra and Nabataean | It looks like Phoenician And |

# Chapter 5
# Inscriptions

Reading these inscriptions is not easy because of the type of rocks used. Firstly, there are sand rocks that are affected by the passage of time because they are fragile, so you will find distortions in them, such as the cutting off of some of their parts or the presence of holes in their surface, which makes reading the letters written in the area of distortion difficult, and there are hard rocks such as alabaster, in which the writing process is very difficult, so it becomes The writing is smooth, and due to nature, some of these letters become distorted.

There are rocks that are easy to write on, such as the rock that we call in Iraq (Hallan stone - for use in building decorations), so the writing process is easy and it resists the weather, like what is used in tombstones.

Therefore, I often find the reader trying to adapt the reading so that the sentence is understandable in his language, but I wanted the reading to be literal, so I do not have the right to interpret what the writer wanted to write, because the language in their time was not exactly what it is now.

Although my reading of some inscriptions in Arabic and Syriac does not give the complete meaning, I want to reach the point:

1- The people of the region must read the inscriptions discovered in their homeland in their language, especially in their local languages. Even if the language used is Aramaic, it differs from one region to another, and this is normal.

Therefore, when the inscriptions written in Aramaic script and discovered in Afghanistan are read in their local language (the indigenous people of the country), the reading will be clearer, and the inscriptions discovered in Persia or… When read in their languages, it will be clearer, and so with the inscriptions written in the Sabaean script discovered in Eritrea, Ethiopia, and Somalia, when read in their local languages, it will be clearer than in Syriac and Arabic, and so on.

2- I wanted to say that my reading of these inscriptions (written in Aramaic, Sabaean, or Gezi script), The language used in it is close to the Syriac language, and if this indicates anything, it indicates that the language used in the region was a mixture of Akkadian, Aramaic, Persian, and the local languages that were in circulation in the region to which the Assyrian, Chaldean, and Achaemenid armies arrived, especially during the period when the Aramaic script was used in them. At that time, the occupier did not need translators, as is the case today, as this coexistence resulted in linguistic mixing.

We should also not look at the issue from a fanatical nationalist point of view. In their time, wars were not nationalistic, nor did they have fanatical nationalist sentiments. Therefore, it is easy for the language of the region to intermingle with the occupier. Despite the greatness of the Assyrian, Chaldean, and Achaemenid empires, they accepted the use of the Aramaic script due to its ease in writing their languages. Therefore, we have to deal with these texts (discovered in our homeland today) as our heritage, and we must preserve them and be proud of them, even if they are not in our language today, as long as they are in our homelands and go back to our ancestors. For example, there are thousands of Aramaic inscriptions discovered in Iraq, Syria, Lebanon, Jordan, Palestine, etc… However, the language used today in the region is Arabic

There are also thousands of inscriptions discovered in Saudi Arabia, Yemen, Eritrea, Ethiopia, Somalia, and... In the Sabaean script, which is not in circulation today?

To demonstrate the extent of the spread of ancient alphabets, let us present some Aramaic, Sabaean, and Geez inscriptions from the region.

# Transliteration of Arabic alphabet into English.

:

| Arabic Letter | Name | Transliteration | Transliteration | Example |
|---|---|---|---|---|
| ا | Alif | A | a, ā (long) | أمل (Amal) - hope |
| ب | Ba | B | b | باب (bab) - door |
| ت | Ta | T | t | تم (tam) - complete |

| Arabic Letter | Name | Transliteration | Transliteration | Example |
|---|---|---|---|---|
| ث | Tha | Th | th (as in "thin") | ثقيل (thaqil) - heavy |
| ج | Jeem | J | j (or g in some dialects) | جبل (jabal) - mountain |
| ح | Ha | H' | ḥ (voiceless, pharyngeal) | حب (hub) - love |
| خ | Kha | Kh | kh (like the German "Bach") | خيل (khayl) - horse |
| د | Dal | D | d | دلو (dalw) - bucket |
| ذ | Dhal | Dh | dh (as in "this") | ذهب (dhahab) - gold |
| ر | Ra | R | r | رأس (ra's) - head |
| ز | Zay | Z | z | زيت (zayt) - oil |
| س | Seen | S | s | سماء (sama') - sky |
| ش | Sheen | Sh | sh | شمس (shams) - sun |
| ص | Saad | S' | ṣ (emphatic s) | صديق (ṣadiq) - friend |

| Arabic Letter | Name | Transliteration | Transliteration | Example |
|---|---|---|---|---|
| ض | Daad | D' | ḍ (emphatic d) | ضوء (ḍaw') - light |
| ط | Taa | T | ṭ (emphatic t) | طريق (ṭariq) - road |
| ظ | Thaa | Z' | ẓ (emphatic dh) | ظهر (ẓuhr) - noon |
| ع | Ayn | A' | ʿ (voiced, pharyngeal) | علم(`ilm) - knowledge |
| غ | Ghayn | Gh | gh (voiced uvular fricative) | غريب (gharib) - strange |
| ف | Fa | F | F | فصل (fasl) - chapter |
| ق | Qaf | Q | q (uvular stop) | قلب (qalb) - heart |
| ك | Kaf | K | K | كتاب (kitab) - book |
| ل | Lam | L | L | ليل (layl) - night |
| م | Meem | M | M | ماء (ma') - water |
| ن | Noon | N | N | نور (nur) - light |

| Arabic Letter | Name | Transliteration | Transliteration | Example |
|---|---|---|---|---|
| هـ | Ha | H | H | هواء (hawa') - air |
| و | Waw | W | w or ū (long u) | ورد (ward) - rose |
| ي | Ya | Y | y or ī (long i) | يوم (yawm) – day |
| ط | g | is "g" in Egyptian Arabic | | |

# Chapter 5
# Aramaic inscriptions
# 1– Inscription from the Iraqi city
# of Nimrud[35]

A TT ivory fragment from room SW 37 in the
Shalmaneser Fortress in Nimrud, inscribed with three
lines in Aramaic script, dating back to the eighth century
BC. The publisher says that it is written in the Hebrew
script, but it is correct that it is in the Aramaic script, and

Nimrud Materialities of Assyrian Knowledge production[35]
https://oracc.museum.upenn.edu/nimrud/ancientkalhu/thewritings/aramaichebr
ew/

perhaps it was in Aramaic and Akkadian, similar to other inscriptions.

The inscription reads:

Right piece:

ن ز ا (و ، ر) ...

( ܗܘ ) ܐܙ / ( ܐ ؟ ܩ ) ܐ ܝ ܢ

N Z A ( N Z A W )
It means: jumped
Maybe:
N Z R / ܢܙܪ
FASTS
The middle piece:

ل ه ف (ب) ت

م م ل ا . ط ي ل ....

ك ح م م . ز ه ،،،

ܠ ܗ ܩ ܗ (ܟ) ܬ

،،،، ܠ , ܝ ، ܐ ܠ ܩ ܩ ܩ

،،، ܗ ܝ ، ܩ ܩ ܝ ܢ

...LH F T
....M M L A . G Y L
Z. M(N) M H' k..

When we read it in Arabic, it does not give meaning, so we will read it in Syriac:

ܠ ܗ ܩ ܗ ( ܠܩܒܬ )

ܒܬܒܒ ܒܠ ܐܟܒܒ

،، ܒܒܒܚ ܗܝ ܢ

Translation:
He has a break (Small piece)

Balanced speech
H Z Inhale it

63

# 2– Bronze duck engraving[36]

It was found in 1989 in the city of Nimrud - Nineveh Governorate by the Iraqi archaeological mission headed by the Iraqi archaeologist Muzahim Mahmoud Hussein Al-Zubaie. On one side there is writing in cuneiform script and on the other side in the Aramaic alphabet, its scholars believe that it dates back to the Assyrian era. Perhaps it is among the possessions of Queen Atalia, wife of the Assyrian King Sargon II (722-705 BC).

They read the Aramaic text:

ش ت ت أ ر ق ا

ܦ ܂ ܐ ܬ ܬ ܫ

SH T T A R Q A

---

36

https://www.facebook.com/zowaa.org/posts/1630978977101285/?locale=ar_A
R

But the first sign is not clear. I do not know if it is the letter (sh) as claimed or if it is an ornament. Likewise, there is no sign symbolizing the letter (a) at the end of the sentence.

If (sh) was read in Syriac:

ܫܬܐ ܐܪܩ

Shatt arq

ܫܬܐ ܐܪܩ

Means:

One-sixth of it becomes thin

Or:

Its bottom is extended

# 3– Inscription from the city of Hatra – Iraq[37]

An inscription from the Iraqi city of Hatra. The publisher did not specify its date, but it dates back to the third century AD.

The inscription reads:

ب ل ه ب

د م د ب ر ك

ل ر ب د

ط ع د م ر ن

ح ل ه ح

ه ق د ب و ى

ܠܝ ܒ ܗ

ܐ ܒ ܗ ܝ ܠ

B  L  H  B
T' M  T' B  R K[38]
L  R  B  D
G  W  B  M  D  Y[39]
When we read it in Arabic, it does not give meaning, so
we will read it in Syriac:

ܒ ܗ ܒ

ܐ ܡ ܐ ܒ ܪ ܟ

ܠܝ ܒ ܗ

ܓ ܘ ܒ ܡ ܕ ܝ

It means:
With flame
He backfills to the news of his kindness / Blessing
blood
To greatness D
The grave of his salvation / Mr. screams /

---

[38] This letter does not resemble the ancient Aramaic, Hadari,
Palmyrene, or Nabataean letters. It reads the Phoenician letter (d), so I will
read it later  as the letter (d) and it resembles the Hadari letter ta
[39] The second letter of the third line reads Phoenician (A) and Syriac (W)

# 4– Inscription from the city of Neyrab, Syria[40]

Basalt funerary stele bearing an Aramaic inscription, ca. Seventh or eighth century BC. Found in Al-Nairab or Tel Avis – Syria, They are two inscriptions in the Aramaic script that were found in 1891 in Nayrab, near Aleppo, Syria. Currently located in the Louvre Museum.

  Mnamon / Ancient writing systems in the Mediterranean Acritical guide to [40] electronic resources
https://mnamon.sns.it/index.php?page=Immagini&id=2&img=640&lang=e
Primary source: S. B. Brock, D. J. K. Taylor, The Hidden Pearl. The Syriac Orthodox Church and its Ancient Aramaic Heritage, 1st edition, Rome 2001, p. 19

The top section reads:

ش ن ي ر ب ن ك م و

ش ه د ب ن د ب م ت

ن ت ن ه  ص ل م ه

ك ا ر  ص ت ه

م ن  ا ت

ت ه ن س  ص م ا

ح ن ه  ر ا د ت

م ن  ا ش د ه

ܫ ܢ ܝ ܪ ܒ ܢ ܟ ܡ ܘ
ܫ ܗ ܕ ܒ ܢ ܕ ܒ ܡ ܬ
ܢ ܬ ܢ ܗ ܨ ܠ ܡ ܗ
ܟ ܐ ܪ ܨ ܬ ܗ
ܡ ܢ ܐ ܬ
ܬ ܗ ܢ ܣ ܨ ܡ ܐ
ܚ ܢ ܗ ܪ ܐ ܪ ܬ
ܡ ܢ ܐ ܫ ܕ ܗ

SH N YR B N K M W
SH H D B N D B M T
N T N H S'L M H
K A R S'T H
M N A T
T H N S S'M A
H'N H R A D T
M N A SH D H

When we read it in Arabic, it does not give meaning, so we will read it in Syriac:

ܫܢܝ ܪܒܢ ܟܡܘ
ܫܗ ܕ ܒܢ ܕܒܡܬ
ܢܬ ܢܗ ܨ ܠܡܗ
ܟܐܪ ܨ ܬܗ
ܡܢ ܐܬ
ܬܗ ܢܣ ܨ ܡܐ
ܚܢ ܗܪܐܪܬ
ܡܢ ܐܫܕܗ

Translation:

He became old the Lord Kimo / the Lord enacted (refined) Kemo

D son Dabamat is tired

He sighed and his face twitched

He scolded his obedience

From his arrival

Delayed, shaken, guard / Delayed disturbance of the guard

Pity, quarrel, tremble

or / bloodshed) ( From falling

The bottom section: There is difficulty in reading the end of each line due to the folding of the person's robe, especially the last line, and perhaps from the beginning of the line. I also missed reading some words. However, the inscription is read from below:

هـ د ن ش م ش م ن ن ل و (م)
ص و و ا ش د و م ر ح ن (...) ن
ع ل و م ي ه ا ب ع و ...
هـ د ص ل م ت م ق د ص ر
ح د ز

ܗܕ ܪ ܝ ܪ ܐ ܪ ܐ ܝ ܗ ܠ ܕ ܗ
ܝ ܘ ܘ ܩ ܐ ܕ ܘ ܟ̈ܪ ܐ ܡ ܪ ܡ̈ ܐ ܠ ܨ
ܘ ܠ ܘ ܕ ܗ ܪ ܡ̇ ܗ ܪ ܟ ܒ ܟ ܠ ܘ ܗ
ܗܕ ܝ ܕ ܪ ܡ ܛ ܪ ܠ ܝ ܗ̇ ܪ ܡ ܕ ܝ ܪ

H D N SH M SH M N N L W (M)
S' W W A SH D W M R H' N N
A' L W M Y H A B A' W ...
H D S' L M T M Q D S' R
H' D Z

When we read it in Arabic, it does not give meaning, so we will read it in Syriac:

Translation:
This tomb is called Nenlu
Installed and believe by Mr. Hanan
The water has risen since the request
This is a maqdser ( maqrsr) statue
Stitches

# 5– Berkop inscription – Zingerli[41]

The Barrkab inscriptions are ten inscriptions in ancient Aramaic and one in a dialect influenced by Canaanite. Some of them are long, some are limited to one word, and all of them are in the Aramaic alphabet of King Barrkab.

[41] https://www.researchgate.net/figure/Bar-Rakib-Palace-Orthostat-1-KAI-216-Photograph-by-Mark-Lester_fig3_360308139

It was found in the city of Shamal (the site of Zengerli - currently Turkey), the capital of the Aramaic Kingdom of Yadi. Dating back to around 730 BC, it is housed in the Museum of the Ancient Orient in Istanbul, catalogued under number 7697.

The text was inscribed on stone (height 1.31 m, width 0.62 m), and decorated the new royal palace built by the King of Shamal. We chose one text to read.

Due to the difficulty of reading, I relied on an inscription published by Daniel Colani[42], a professor at the Hebrew

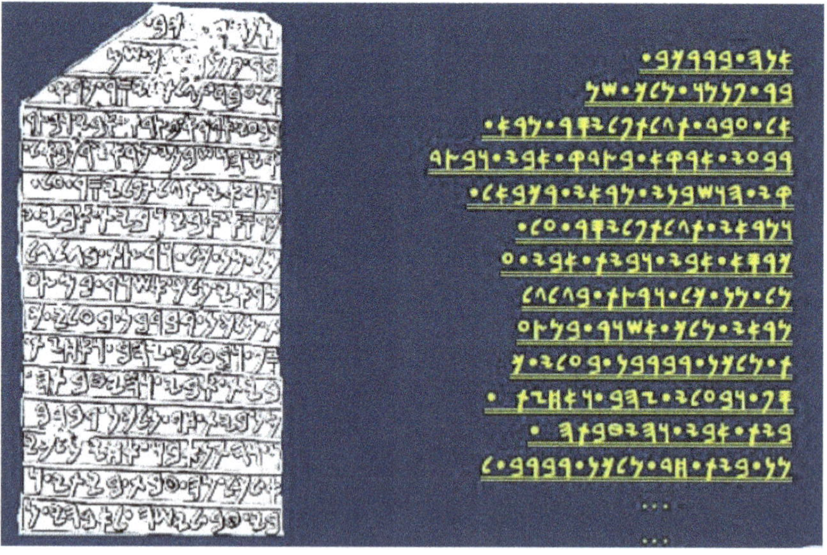

University in Jerusalem   The inscription comprises twenty lines, but Daniel published only thirteen, based on

[42] https://www.pinterest.com.au/pin/351773420870408021/

an image of the original that shows sixteen lines. There are three lines that he did not read, which are:

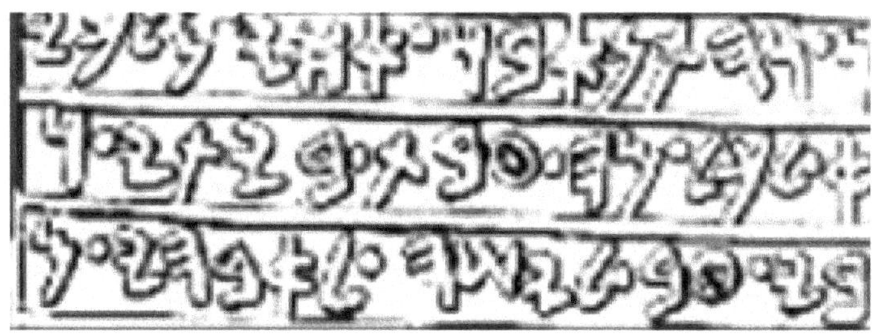

There are four more lines left, which I quoted from Professor Mahmoud Al-Ash (Mahmoud Al-Atassi) - Professor of Semitic Languages at the University of Aleppo, who published his reading of the inscription via Google in the form of a video through the link:

https://www.youtube.com/watch?v=wrQ1XJdxbnA

The inscription reads:

ا ن هـ. ب ر ر ك ب .

ب ر . ط ن م و . م ل ك . ش م

ا ل . ع ب د . ت ط ل ت ف ل ي س ر ا . م ر ا

ر ب ع ي . ا ر ق ا . ب ص د ق . ا ب ي . و ب ص ر

ق ي . هـ و ش ب ن ي . م ر ا ي . ر ك ب ا ل .

و م ر ا ي . ت ط ل ت ف ل ي س ر ر . ع ل .

ك ر س ا . ا ب ي . و ب ي ت . ا ب ي . ع

م ل . م ن . ك ل . و ر ص ت . ب ط ل ط ل

م ر ا ي . م ل ك . ا ش و ر . ب م ص ع

ت . م ل ك ن . ر ب ر ب ن . ب ع ل ي . ك

س ف . و ب ع ل ي . ي هـ ب . و ا ح ي ت

ب ي ت . ا ب ي . و هـ ي ط ب ت ت هـ .

م ن . ر ي ت . ح د . م ل ك ن . ر ب ر ب . ل

ن . ع و هـ ت . ا ب و ا ح ي , ا ح ي . م ل ك ي

ا . ل ك ل . م ه . ط ب ت . ب ي ت ي . و

ب ي . ط ب . ل ي ش ه . ل ا ب ه ي . م

ل ك ي . ش م ا ل . ه ا . ب ي ت . ك ل م

و . ل ه م . ف ه ا . ب ي ت . ش ت و ا . ل

ه م . و ه ا . ب ي ت . ك ي ص ا . و

ا ن ه . ب ن ي ت . ب ي ت ا . ز ن ه

A N H . B R R K B

B R . G N M W . M L K . SH M

A L . A’ B D . T G L T F L Y S R . M R A
R B A’ Y . A R Q A , B S’ D Q . A B Y . W B S’ R
Q Y . H W SH B N Y . M R A Y . R K B A L
W M R A Y . T G L T F L Y S R . A’ L
K R S A . A B Y . W B E T . A B Y . A’
M L . M N . K L . W R S’ T . B G L G L
M R A Y . M L K . A SH W R . B M S’ A’
T . M L K N . R B R B N . B A’ L Y . K
S F . W B A’ L Y . Y H B . W A H’ Y T
B Y T . A B Y . W H Y T’ B T H
M N . R E T . H’ D . M L K N . R B R B . L
N . W H T . A B W . A H’ Y . M L K Y
A . L K L . M H . T’ B T . B Y T Y . W
B Y . T’ B . L Y SH H . L A B H Y . M
L K Y . SH M A L H A . B Y T . K L M
W . L H M . F H A . B Y T . SH T W A . L
H M . W H A . B Y T . K Y S’ A . W
A N H . B N Y T . B Y T A . Z N H

When we read it in Arabic, it does not give meaning, so
we will read it in Syriac:

ܐܢܟ ܒܪܪ ܟܦ

ܒܪ ܓܢܡܘ ܡܠܟ ܫܡܐܠ

ܥܒܕܗ ܕܬܓܠܬܦܠܣܪ ܡܪܐ

ܐܬܚܒ ܐܪܣܝ ܘܗܝ ܛܐܒ ܚܣܕ ܐܒܝ

Translation:
I'm Brr Kp
Son Ghanmo, King of Shamal
The servant of Tiglath-Pileser the Master
My bed was extended, the kindness of my father was
tender, and is small

Why did my sir capture me?[43]
And my master, Tiglat Fleiser,
He rode on my father's throne and my father's house
Was tender, and he was small
Make all the chicks by rotating
Sir, King of Assyria
By our King is the Lord of our Lord, Bali
Silver and my God bestows life
My father's house and his virtue
From the house of one of our kings, great god
What, the father of my king's brother
For everything that is good for my home and
With good news to his fathers
With the news of the dough to his fathers
My king Shmal, behold the house of Calmo
For the confusion of his wandering (bewilderment),
winter house (below)[44]
For turmoil, this is, (His name, the Almighty) came to
plaster house and
I built this type

---

[43] The literal translation of the original text of the three verses is:
Why did he capture me, sir, I rode the ..
And my master, Tiglat, will be pleased with me
My Father's throne and my Father's house
[44] Perhaps it is (ܣܬܘܐ – Stoa/winter) and it is more correct

# 6– Inscription from the city of Petra, Jordan[45]

It has a break on the right side and there is a disfigurement in the last letters of the last line.

---

[45] Petra– The Good, the Bad, and the Ugly

https://travelswithdan.com/2017/09/20/petra-the-good-the-bad-and-the-ugly/

The inscription reads:

ا ش ر د ك ن ح

.. ن ك ي ف د س د ك ف ر ش ي ا

ع (هـ) ل ح ن ن ح ر ت ت

ط ف ف ه ت د ف م ن ت ص (ش)

م ن د ف م ن ع ن ب ط ف

ع ح ف ر د ص ن ف ه د

ش ن ت ف ....

A SH R D K N H'
.. N K Y F D S D K F R SH Y A
A'(H) L H' N N H' R T T
T' F F H T D F M N T S'(SH)
M N D F M N A' N B T' F
A' H' F R D S' N F H D
SH N T F ...

When we read it in Arabic, it does not give meaning, so
we will read it in Syriac:

Translation:

Extraction (stray), blocking h'
N concealing the spread of great disbelief
We have to plowing T
The board was overflowing with conflict
From the tablet, from the clouds, it floated
A' digging monument banished d
Year 80

# 7– Two graffiti from Ain Shalala cave in Jordan[46]

In Wadi (Valley) Rum, a series of Aramaic–Nabataean inscriptions was discovered near sacred sites, including the Ain Shalalah temple—a cave nestled high in the rocky cliffs. It contains 27 inscriptions, all in the Nabataean language except for 2 in Greek.

Because the image of the inscription is not clear, I had to rely on the publisher's reading of the inscription, and I was unable to confirm the accuracy of the reading.

---

[46] SOME NOTIONS ABOUT THE PRE-ISLAMIC INSCRIPTIONS OF THE JORDANIAN DESERTS (AND  BEYOND ...
https://www.pathsofjordan.net/the-rock-art/some-notions-about-the-pre-islamic-inscriptions-of-the-jordanian-deserts-and-beyond

The upper part reads:

د ك ر ت ط ل ت و ب ر ط م ي

ب ر ق ي م ت ب ن ي ط ر و

ش م ز ق و ر و ن ي ب

ܕܚܘ ܗ ܐܠ ܬܗܘܒ ܪܛܡܝ ܕ,

ܟܘܡ,ܩ ܬܗ, ܒܚܠ ܪ,ܠ ,,,

ܫܡܙܩܘܪܘܢܝܒ ,

When we read it in Arabic, it does not give meaning, so
we will read it in Syriac:

ܕܚܘ ܗ ܐܠ ܬܗܘܒ ܪܛܡܝ ܕܠܚܪ

ܟܢ ܡܚܫܐ ܚܕܪ ܠܢ ,,,

ܫܡ ܘܡܘܪܘ ܢܝܒ

Translation:

It mention, he shade his regret, Ratmi
The son of Qaymat and the Tar family...
He named the zaqqur and ivory


The bottom reads:

د ك ر ت ط ل ت ع ي ر و
ب ن ي ط ن ر (د) ط ن ش ل م ...

D K R T T' L T A' Y R W
B N Y T' N R (D) T' N SH L M...

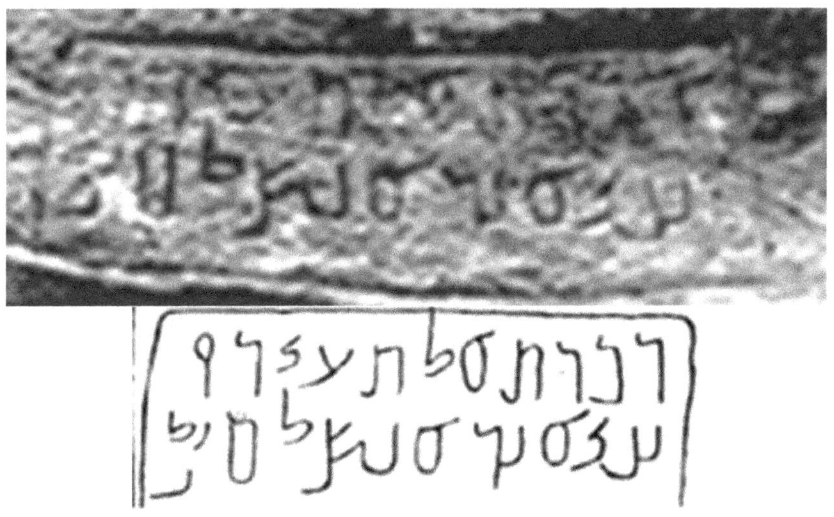

When we read it in Arabic, it does not give meaning, so
we will read it in Syriac:

87

Translation:
It is mentioned that he shade taaero
The son of Yatan complains of peace

# 8– Corozin inscription from Palestine[47]

An inscription was discovered in the village of Corozin, near the Sea of al-Jalil. It is believed to mark the seat of Moses. The writing is unclear. I could read part of the first line.

... ا ط ن ي ب ر

ﻥ ﻤ ﻠ ﻄ ﺔ

---

[47] Chorozaïne, jumelle maudite!https://www.interbible.org/interBible/decouverte/archeologie/2000/ar c_000915.htm

R B Y N T' A …
In the Arabic language (Rabe nta) means (My Lord has given)

ܐܢ ܒܠ ܟ

But at Syriac language means (My Lord has moisten)
But the third letter resembles the letter H of Tadmur so the text can be read:

ܐܢ ܒܠܣ

Translation:
My Lord, shine

# 9. Aramaic inscription from Jerusalem[48]

A stone column was recently discovered in Jerusalem excavations. This inscription dates back to the 1st century BC.
The inscription is distorted, so it is difficult to read some of its letters. So the scribe draws some of its letters in Hebrew script, and most of them are ancient Aramaic, so the inscription is read:

(...) و ب ن ط ح ط ز ن

و ط م و هـ ...

---

48 Some Notable First-Century BCE Palestinian Jews With Greek Names
https://mosaicmagazine.com/observation/history-ideas/2018/10/some-notable-first-century-bce-palestinian-jews-with-greek-names/

م ط ن ط ش ...

(...) W B N G  H' G Z N
W G M W H ...
M G N G SH ...
When we read it in Arabic, it does not give meaning, so
we will read it in Syriac:

Translation:


The son of gah' is our wealth
And lots of wh...
Free test

# 10– Clay inscription from the Pula region[49]

[49] Bible Artifacts Found Outside the Trench: Israelite Clay Bullae
https://www.biblicalarchaeology.org/daily/biblical-artifacts/artifacts-and-the-bible/israelite-clay-bullae/

This clay seal, or bulla, is one of many ancient clay balls uncovered through excavations and appearing on the antiquities market, where it was photographed by Robert Deutsch.  It dates back to the period (597-587) BC and is written in the ancient Aramaic script. It has been broken on the right and bottom sides. Its researchers read the first line (Shabna) and believed that it was the word Shebnyahu.

This type of writing on clay balls was widely used by the Sumerians.

The inscription is read:

... ز ش ب ن (ح) هـ ط

... هـ م ز ن (ت )

... Z SH B H' H K
H M Z T
We will read it in Syriac:

Translation:
Z praise and contemplates
... Spoke / despicable ZT
Because of the breakage, the meaning is unclear

# 11– Phoenician inscription from Lebanon[50]

[50] National Museum of Beirut
From Wikipedia, the free encyclopedia
https://en.wikipedia.org/wiki/National_Museum_of_Beirut

A Phoenician limestone sundial with an inscription, dating back to the Hellenistic period, the fourth century BC.

There is difficulty in reading the inscription, as the writing is not clear due to the type of rock used.

The inscription reads:

ن ت ا ن م ح ن ق ... ع .... و ص ع ا ... ل ن ط

G N L ... A A' S' W ... A' ... Q N H' M N A T N

When we read it in Arabic, it does not give meaning, so we will read it in Syriac:

Translation:

Lie down L.. A force w.. A'.. Nathan's eagerness subsides

# 12– Inscription from the Byblos region[51]

This relief is a small continuous fragment of a large vase, or perhaps a wall relief dating back to 900 BC, published in Maurice Dunand's book (Fouilles de Byblos - vol. 2, 1926-1932). Dunand described it as the second landmark in the history of the alphabet between the Middle Kingdom of Egypt and the reign of the King of Byblos, Ahiram. Before 1933, it was found in the Byblos region, Keserwan-Jbeil, Lebanon.

It has a broke on the right and the bottom, and the drawing of the letters in many of them is confusing because they do not resemble the drawing of the Phoenician or Aramaic letters that are familiar to them, perhaps due to the attempt of the discoverer (reader) of the inscription to pass his pen over these marks.

---

[51] From Wikipedia, the free encyclopedia
https://en.wikipedia.org/wiki/Abda_sherd

The inscription is read from left to right according to the
lettering:

هـ ط هـ بـ لـ ... بـ ز كـ ا ب

or:

H G H B L .. B Z K A B

When we read it in Arabic, it does not give
meaning, so we will read it in Syriac:

or:

Translation:
Contemplate falsehood… Stealing sadness
Or:
Polite but… Stealing sadness

# 13– Aramaic inscription from Saudi Arabia[52]

An Aramaic inscription on an incense burner, dating back to about 600 BC. It is located in the Saudi National Museum, Riyadh. It is distorted from the bottom.

---

It is noted that the writer of the inscription did not adhere to a fixed drawing of the calligraphy; some of the letters are confusing among them:
It only slightly resembles the Aramaic letter (h'),   so I will read it (h')

It looks like the Phoenician letter (d), so I'll read it 
as (d).
It does not resemble any of the Phoenician or
Aramaic letters.
The inscription reads:

ح ح ن ن ت ن ن ي

ق و ب ن د .. (Phoenician) ن ح

ب و ت ن ش ن

... ن ح ت ن

... ن ح ي ي

.... و ط ن ن ب ش

H' H' N N T N Y
Q W B N D .. N H'
B W T N SH N
... N H' T N
... N H' Y Y
... W G N N B SH

101

When we read it in Arabic, it does not give
meaning, so we will read it in Syriac:

ܕ ܣܝ ܠܗܝ

ܘܩܒ ܢ: "" ܣܝ

ܩܘܗ ܢܥ

"" ܣܝܠܝ

"" ܣܝܣܝ

( ܢܗܥ ) ܢܚܥ ܠܝ ܘ ""

Translation:
H pity, talk
Sagittarius is fed up .. NH'
Regarding our women
… incline
… ….we salute
... And planting, dig

# 14– Madain Saleh inscription[53]

A sundial inscription carved from red sandstone, likely linked to astronomical use, was discovered in the city of Mada'in Saleh in Saudi Arabia. It bears Aramaic script

---

[53] A Nabataean Sundial from Mada'in Salih
  John F. Healey
https://www.persee.fr/doc/syria_0039-7946_1989_num_66_1_7115

and dates back to the first century BC. It is now in the Museum of the Ancient East - Istanbul Archaeological Museums under the number 7664.

The writing is not clear, so it is difficult to distinguish the letters.

The inscription reads:

م ز ط هـك ي و ز ن ز ق و ح

M Z G H K Y W Z N Z Q W H'
When we read it in Arabic, it does not give meaning, so we will read it in Syriac:

Translation:
Here the tiger mix up and shouted
OR:
M Z G SH K Y Z Y N Z Q Z H'

Translation:
Here the tiger jumped and shouted

# 15– Aramaic inscription from Egypt[54]

This inscription is called (the Carpentras Inscription) and it was the first Aramaic inscription to be published in Europe in the French city of Carpentras. It was discovered and published by Professor M. Rigord in 1704.

The text is written on a limestone plaque, and it is from the late Achaemenid era, i.e. the fifth century BC.

The publisher read it:

Recto


The Nabataean script : A bridge between the Aramaic and the [54]
Arabic Alphabets
https://www.pathsofjordan.net/some-facts-about-the-nabataeans/the-nabataean-script-a-bridge-between-the-aramaic-and-the-arabic-alphabets

l. 1) k'n hlw ḥlm
l. 2) 1 ḥzyt wmn
l. 3) 'dn' hw 'nh
l. 4) ḥmm šg'
l. 5) [']tḫzy ḥz[w]
l. 6) mlwhy l. 7) šlm

Verso

l. 1) k'n hn ṣbty
l. 2) kl tzbny hmw l. 3) y'klw ynqy' l. 4) hlw l' l. 5) š'r
l. 6) qṭyn

The inscription reads:
Right side:

م ي ن ط ل د ح ل م

ط ز ز م ن ر ك ب

و و ز ت ع ر و ص ..

ح م م ش ط ي و

ص ح ز ع ز و و

م ل و هـ ي

ز ل م

M  Y N G L D H' L M
G Z Z M N R K B
W W Z T A' R W S' ...
H' M M SH G Y W
S' H' Z A' Z W W
 M L W H Y
Z L M

When we read it in Arabic, it does not give meaning, so
we will read it in Syriac:

ܗܡ ܚܠܕ ܣܠܡ
ܟܠܐ ܗܡ ܐܚܕ
ܩܘܡ ܚܬ ܗܝ
ܣܚܡ ܥܠܡ ܘ
ܝܝ ܐܚ ܐܩ ܐ
ܗܠ ܗܗ ܝ
ܐܠܡ

Translation:
Our water frozen and delicious
Fewer passengers
And the goose got bored and attacked
Heated, choked and…
Clear d, isturbed (moved), swollen…
He filled and she swerves

The left side reads:

ا ص ب و ز ع ز و ن
(د) ر م ع ز ر ز ب ت ل ط
ح و ن ب ر ل د و ز ط
ا ل د ل ع
ز و..ز ن ش
ب و ط ن

ܝܘܩܝܚܘܩܒ ܟ
ܟܥܝܝܢܩܒܬܗܠ ܡ
ܐ ܗܩܢܒܬܗ ܢܘܚ
ܚ ܠܕ ܠ ܟ

N W Z A' Z W B S' A
G L T Z B R Z R A' M R(D)
G Z W D L R B N W H'
A' L D L A
SH Z... W Z
N T' W B

We read it in Syriac:

Translation:
He dispute and became heated and research
Revolted and heated the son Zara'm R...
Noah's master became dry and humiliated
He entered without
... Goose
Boredom

# 16– Aramaic inscription from Taxila – India[55]

[55] Aramaic inscription of Taxila
From Wikipedia, the free encyclopedia
https://www.wikiwand.com/en/Aramaic_inscription_of_Taxila

It is an inscription on a piece of marble, discovered by Sir John Marshall in 1915 in Sarkab - Pakistan (formerly Taxila - British India).

An inscription written in Aramaic, dating back to the third or fourth century BC. Published by John Marshall in Calcutta, India in 1918.

The publisher says that Aramaic was the official language of The Achaemenes Empire, which disappeared in 330 BC with the conquests of Alexander the Great. It seems that this inscription was addressed directly to the inhabitants of this ancient empire that still exists in northwestern India.

The discovery of this inscription was followed by the discovery of several other inscriptions in Aramaic or Greek (or both), written by King Ashoka. The most famous of these is the bilingual Kandahar rock inscription, written in both Greek and Aramaic called - Ashoka's Greek Edict - of Kandahar.

In 1932, another inscription in Aramaic was discovered in Wadi Laghman in Poli Darunta. Then in 1963, an inscription was discovered in the "Indo-Aramaic" language, alternating between the Indic language and the Aramaic language, but using the Aramaic script only, and the Aramaic parts translated the Indian parts written in the Aramaic alphabet. Also found in Kandahar. Finally, another inscription was found in Laghman, the Aramaic Laghman inscription.

In fact, reading the inscription is difficult because the image of the original is unclear. Relying on the publisher's drawing is also problematic, as he used a mix of scripts—including ancient Aramaic, Nabataean, Palmyrene, Hebrew, and Hatra—to shape the letters.

The inscription reads:

ز ك و ر ق ...

ل د (ر) م ط ن ص ط ه ل

ن ط ي ر ص ت ه ل

ت ن ز و ش ب ط ي ر ص ت

د ل ت ب ر ه ي ه د ر

ه ر د ص ي ح (م) ص ه ز ي ح

ز ن ي م ر د ن ر (د) م

م ر ي ش ص ب ن ز ط م ر ص

ا ي ت ن و ر ن ر د

ح (م) ل ن ر ص

ر ت و ي ن ر ح ي

ل م ن ت ن و د ط ن ن

Z K W R Q
L D(R) M G N S' G H L
N G Y R S' T H L
T N Z W SH B G Y R S' T
D L T B R H Y H D R
H R D S' Y H'(M) S' H Z Y H'
Z N Y M R D N R(D) M
M R Y SH S' B N Z G M R S'
A Y T N W R N R D
H'(M) L N R S'
R T W Y N R H' Y
L M N T N W D T' N N

When we read it in Arabic, it does not give meaning, so we will read it in Syriac:

ܙܟܘܪ ܩ ‘‘‘
ܠܕܡ (ܠܪܡ) ܓܢܥ ܓܗܠ
ܢܓܝܪ ܥܬ ܗܠ
ܬܢ ܙܘ ܫܒ ܓܝܪܥܬ
ܕܠ ܬܒܪ ܗܝ ܗܕܪ
ܗܪܕ ܥܝܚ (ܥܡ) ܥܗ ܙܝܚ
ܙܢܝ ܡܪܕܢ ܪܡ (ܕܡ)
ܡܪ ܫܥ ܒܢ ܙܓ ܡܪܥ
ܐܝܬ ܢܘܪ ܢܪܕ
ܚܠ (ܡܠ) ܢܪܥ
ܪܬܘ ܝܢܪ ܚܝ
ܠܡܢ ܬܢ ܘܕ ܛܢܢ

Translation:
The fortune teller Q
For height (for lineage) he despise and raging
Publish Listen and cheered
The smoke tends and lighted grinding
The glory was broken
Demolish his fasting (cry), thirst, and celebrate
He classified our rebellion as his reform (blood)
Mr. Yass the son of Zak scrub
Our fire walking
Our dust is crushed
The living yenner trembled
For those who smoke, N be ashes

# 17– The Kandahar rock inscription is bilingual[56]

The Kandahar rock inscription, which is bilingual (Greek and Aramaic), dates back to the third century BC. It was

From Wikipedia, the free encyclopedia[56]
https://en.wikipedia.org/wiki/Aramaic

found in Afghanistan in the form of a monument erected by King Asoka (or Ashoka) in Kandahar. According to what was discovered by the discoverers of these inscriptions and historians, Asoka corresponded with the Hellenistic rulers, including Ptolemy II Philadelphus (the second king of the Ptolemaic state who ruled Egypt from 283 BC to 246 BC) in Alexandria. This raises several questions: Was Asoka's language Aramaic or because Aramaic was still the official language in the region at that time?

The inscription consists of fourteen lines in Greek and eight lines in Aramaic. There is difficulty in reading and translating the Aramaic text because many of the letters are not clear, so we need to go back to the original inscription, which may be in Indian museums.

To read it and know its language, whether the Aramaic text was in Hindi, Persian, Greek, or perhaps Aramaic

The inscription reads:

1- ش و ن ... ك ت ط ت د ز ص ز ي ط و ش ك ز و ل ز ن ي
و ط هـ م ل و ي ز م هـ.. ل ك ...
2- ... و ر ز و ط ر ز ... ط و م ن ي ك ل ط ن ب ز ن و ن و
ي م ... ن ش ن .. و ل هـ و ز ل ز و .. ش ...
3- ر .. و ط .. ك م .. ط ك ش ز ر ت ك ل ط ز .. م ي ... ت ل ك ن
و و ص و ... ل ..

4- .. ط ح ل ط م ل ك م ز هـ د(ر) ل هـ ن هـ ن ش ن د(ر) ت ص هـ ط
ز ك ز د ك ز ي ...
5- ا ن ب(ر) ق ص ش ن د(ر) .. ط ز ن ص و ن و ز ط ط ن .. ك
ص م ط ل ن ن .. ز ن هـ م ك ز ن ...

6- ط ن ط م هـ د(ر) ك ي ز ك م ط م ص ط ل ت ن ع د(ر) هـ ا د(ر)
ل .. ب ط م ط د ل ك ل ط ص ط .... ش د(ر)

7- ت ط ن ع و د(ر) هـ .. د(ر) ش ... ت ز ص ا ب .. أ و ط ... د(ر)
م ت ن ش .. و ...

8- ... م ن .. ف ح ط د (ر) ل هـ م ي ش .. د(ر) ... د(ر) ط هـ ز ص
ك ....

1- ...

2- ...

3- ...

4- ...

5- ...

6- ...

7- ...

8- ...

SH W N .. K T G T D Z S' Z Y G W SH K Z W L Z N
Y W G H M L W Y Z M H .. L K
... W R Z W G R Z ... G W M N Y K L G N B Z N W
N W Y M ... N SH N .. W L H W Z L Z W ... SH ...
R .. W T' ... K M ... G K SH Z R T K L G Z ... M Y ..
T L K N W W S' W ... L ..

..G H'L G M L K M Z H D (R) L H N H N SH D(R) T S' H G Z K Z D K Z Y
A N B(R) Q S'SH N D(R) .. G Z N S'W N W Z G G N .. K S'M G L N .. Z N H M K Z N ..
G N T'M H D(R) K Y Z K M T'M S'G L T N A' D(R) H A D(R) L .. B G M T' D L K L G S'G ... SH D(R) T G N A'W D(R) H .. D(R) SH ... T Z S' A B ... A W G ... D(R) M T N SH ... W ...
... M N .. F H'G D(R) L H M Y SH ... D(R) ... D(R) G H Z S'K ...

It is difficult to read because there are missing letters within the lines.

# 18– Aramaic inscription from Abkhazia[57]

Archaeologists from Abkhazia and Russia, working on an expedition near the cities of Tkuarchal and Ochamchira in Abkhazia, have uncovered a fragment of an ancient stela bearing an Aramaic inscription, along with other texts, according to publisher Barjandzia. According to scholars, its history dates back to approximately the sixth century and others to the fourth century.

However, whether this date is meant after AD is questionable, as the Aramaic script disappeared centuries

---

[57] An ancient plate with inscriptions in Aramaic was found during archaeological excavations on the outskirts of modern Ochamchira in Abkhazia.
Said Bargandzhia
https://abaza.org/en/ancient-plate-with-inscriptions-in-aramaic-discovered-in-abkhazia

before that and was replaced by the Syriac script with cursive letters. Therefore, it must either be in the sixth or fourth century BC, and this is more correct because the writer used the ancient Aramaic alphabet, or we have to repeat it. Consider history.

Others considered it Armenian. Perhaps the language is Armenian, but the script is ancient Aramaic[58].

There is difficulty in reading the inscription because some of the letters are not clear due to the discoverer or reader using ink that spreads on the pottery piece, distorting the letter.

The inscription reads:

ت ل ب ط ح (...) ص ر ب ش

ه ل د ڪ س ي د ه

T L B G H' S' R B SH
When we read it in Arabic, it does not give meaning, so we will read it in Syriac:

ه ل ڪ س ي د ه

Translation:

The hill repulsed and tightened (tons)
bsh..

---

58

https://www.facebook.com/ancientarmeniakingdomofgods/photos/a.23225567
31322908/2383772058534708/?type=3

# 19– Inscription from Armenia[59]

Aramaic inscriptions on boundary stones from Armenia, Artaxiad era (3rd-2nd c. BC).

Dozens of stelae up to 1 meter high, with tri-toothed or rounded upper parts, were found in Armenia belonging to the Armenian Artasiad dynasty. The front side of these panels contains carved inscriptions consisting of several lines in the Imperial Aramaic script.

There is difficulty in reading, as the drawing of some letters is confusing, and you will not find anything similar to them in the Imperial Aramaic script. You may find something similar to that in other fonts, and this contradicts the drawing of the same letter on the other hand, since that letter falls within the scope of the Imperial Aramaic letters. Other letters are not clearly

---

59 Who were the Urartians? – The language – [Part 4]
https://www.peopleofar.com/2022/04/09/who-were-the-urartians-part-4/

defined, so we need the original inscription instead of the published image.

The inscription on the right reads:

او ر ز ن ل ق ك س ن و

ب و ز ر هـ و ي د ز و

فـ ر ز و و ز ح لـ ...

.. ت طـ و ي ن

.. طـ و ا

A W R Z N L Q K S N W
B W Z R H W Y D Z W
F R Z W W Z H'L …
.. T T' W Y N
… T' W A

When we read it in Arabic, it does not give meaning, so we will read it in Syriac:

Translation:
Our men was paddle coral
In his field, the hand was down
He fled, retreated and crawled
…We are grilling

Grill

The inscription in the middle:

ا و ... ح ط م

م ن و ب و ز ا

ز و هـ ح و

و ن ن ت و ن ح ن ن

A  W... H' T' M
M  N  W  B  W  Z  A
Z  W  H  H' W
W  N  N  T  W  N  H' N  N
When we read it in Arabic, it does not give meaning, so
we will read it in Syriac:

Translation:
And… Destroy
Who is Boza...
retreat H'w
 And the hymn is tired,
The inscription on the left reads:

123

‫.... و ن‬
‫ط ن ز ر ز ن هـ ن ي و ن ن ي ط ط ي ن ز ن ز‬
‫ط و ز ي ر ص ي ط ر ي ع ط ي ن و‬
‫ي ز م و ن ن ط ي ن ن ر ص ط و ي ص ي ن‬
‫... و ز ح ر ن و ز ن ب ر ز و ن و ...‬
‫.. ك .. و ن ز ز ن و ر ز ...‬

.. W N

T' N Z R Z N H N Y W N N Y G G Y N W Z

N Z

G W Z Y R S' Y T' R Y A' T' Y N W

Y Z M W N N T' Y N N R S' G W Y S' Y N

.. W Z H' R N W Z N B R Z W N W ...

.... K.. W N Z Z N W R Z..

When we read it in Arabic, it does not give meaning, so we will read it in Syriac:

124

Translation:
... W N „„

Connect our symbol, so he delicious, Nane, gagi, screamed, jumped

My nut tree crushed, expelled and erased No…

Yazmo moisturizes and crushes in the tribes

… He removed the rang and type of the seller's son and..

…k… and Ne Diversify the field[60]


## 20- Aramaic Bokan Tepe inscription from Iran[61]

---

[60] Perhaps it is (ܘܪܙܐ ;ܪܘܙܢ - warza,wrazan) meaning the field of watermelon , used by us.

[61] An ancient Aramaic inscription from western Iran / Prof. Dr. Farouk Ismail - Professor at the Free University of Berlin
Journal of the Saudi Society for Archaeological Studies / Studies in the World of Archeology and Heritage / Issue February 2020 AD

A broken stone stele was found from Qalaishi containing 13 lines of engraved Aramaic inscriptions. The so-called Bokan Tepe obelisk in West Azerbaijan Province - Iran dates back to the early eighth century BC on the basis of paleontology.

This inscription is written at the bottom of a huge stone monument in two fragments. The main first was found in 1985 AD at the Qalaiji site near the town of Bokan. Then the second, smaller one appeared in the antiquities market in Tehran in 1990 AD.

The monument is preserved in the Tehran Museum and was published for the first time by the Iranian researcher Rasoul Bashash Kanzaq in the Persian language in 1996. It was translated by Professor Dr. Farouk Ismail, and researchers agree on its date in the second half of the eighth century BC.

The original inscription does not exist, and I do not know how correctly the transfer and drawing of the letters and commas (.) are correct, so I have to rely on the reading of the publisher (or translator). Also, the Arabic translation seemed to me to be a modification.

The inscription reads:

ـه ن ز (ا) ب ص ن . ت ي ا . س ن ـه ي . ي ز -1
ا ن ت و م . ـه م . ك ل م ش ب . و ا . ـه م ح ل ب -2
ب . ن ـه ل ا . ـه و م ش ي . ا ق ر ا . ل ك ب . ـه و ـه . ي ز -3
ص ل و . ن ـه ل ا ل . ا ـه . ص ل و . ا و ـه . ا (ت) ك ل م . ت -4
. ـه ر و ش . ع ب ش . ر ت ع ز ب . ي ز. ي د ل ح ل ا . ـه -5
ب ش و . ع ب ش ي . ل ا و . د ح ل ط ع .ن ق ن ي ـه ي -6
ا ل م ي . ل ا و . د ح ر ن ت ب . و ف ا ي . ن ش ن . ع -7

8- و هـ ي . و ي ا ب د .م ن . م ت هـ . ت ن ن . ا ش هـ . و ق ل
9- ر ح ي ن . و ا ر ق هـ . ت ه و ي . م م ل ح هـ . و ي ت م ر
10- د هـ . ف ر ع . ر ا ش . و م ل ك ا . هـ ا . ز ي (ك ت) ب.
11- ع ل . ن ص ب ا . ز ن هـ . ك ر س ا هـ . ي ه ف ك هـ . هـ د
12- و ح ل د ي . و ش ب ع . ش ن ن . ا ل . ي ت ن . ح ص ر . ق ر ب (ت)
13- ب م ت هـ . و ي م ح ا هـ ي . ك ل . ل و ص . ن ص ب ا . ز ن هـ.

ܙܝ[62]، ܝܗܢܣ(ܢܢ)[63]، ܐܝܬ، ܢܨܒܐܙܢܗ
ܒܠܚܩܗ، ܐܘ، ܒܫܠܡ، ܟܠ، ܡܗ، ܡܘܬܢܐ
ܙܝ، ܗܘܗ، ܒܟܠ، ܐܪܥܐ، ܝܫܩܘܗ، ܐܠܗܢ، ܒ
ܬ، ܡܠܟܬܐ، ܗܘܐ، ܘܠܨ، ܗܐ[64]، ܠܐܠܗܢ، ܘܠ
ܨ
ܗܐ، ܠܚܠܕܝ، ܙܝ، ܒܝܟܬܪ، ܫܒܟ، ܫܘܪܗ
ܝܗܝܢܡܢ، ܟܓܠ، ܚܕ، ܘܐܠ، ܝ[65]ܫܒܟ، ܘܫܒܟ
ܢܫܢ، ܝܐܦܘ، ܒܬܢܪ، ܚܕ، ܘܐܠ، ܝܡܠܐ
ܘܗܝ، ܘܝܐܒܕ، ܡܢ، ܡܬܗ، ܬܢܢ، ܐܫܗ، ܘܩܠ
ܪܚܝܢ، ܘܐܪܩܗ، ܬܗܘܝ، ܡܡܠܚܗ، ܘܝܬܡܪ
ܪܗ، ܦܪܥ، ܪܐܫ، ܘܡܠܟܐ، ܗܐ، ܙܝ...
ܥܠ، ܢܨܒܐ، ܙܢܗ (ܙܢܐ)، ܟܪܣܐܗ (ܟܪܡܐ
ܗ)[66]، ܝܗܦܟܗ، ܗܕ
ܘܚܠܕܝ؛ ܘܫܒܥ، ܫܢܢ، ܐܠ، ܝܬܢ، ܚܨܪ، ܩܪܒܬ
ܒܡܬܗ، ܘܝܡܚܐܗܝ، ܟܠ، ܠܘܨ، ܢܨܒܐ، ܙܢܗ

---

[62] (This word does not exist in Syriac. It may mean (this (zy - ܙܝ)

[63] NN) according to the drawing the letter, - ܢ) The most correct, the word is which means to sing, to recite

[64] An alert letter meaning behold, since (Ha– ܗܐ)

[65] This letter is read as (y), but perhaps it is another letter and perhaps it is a deformation in a piece of rock

[66] The correct one is (M) and not (S) as read by the reader of the inscription

Therefore, I will re-read the inscription in Syriac, which I see as closer to the language of the inscription, and translate it.

Translation:

1- This Lord sang the existence of this monument

67 ,, (This word does not exist in Syriac. It may mean (this (zy - ,, )

68 NN) according to the drawing the letter, - ﺮ) The most correct, the word is which means to sing, to recite

69 An alert letter meaning behold, since (Ha– ܗܐ)

70 This letter is read as (y), but perhaps it is another letter and perhaps it is a deformation in a piece of rock

71 The correct one is (M) and not (S) as read by the reader of the inscription

2- By His bread (by His promise) or by His peace for all our dead

3- This one was affectionately called our God B..

4-… T The queen was a spark, behold, for our God and a spark[72]

5- Behold, because of my creeping (because of my disappearance), this hole has its seven walls cut off[73]

6- My God,  sacrificed, one turn, but  Y seven and seven

7- Our women bake with one oven and it is not full

8- And she, as the smoke disappeared from her village, the smoke subsided and diminished

9- Our mill, abandoned its pollution and dried it

10- Watch. the leader and the king,gave a reward. Behold this …

11- On the accusative, typeing of generosity, he spoils (destroys) this

12- H'lde and seven of us were besieged and brought close

13- His village and erases every distortion of the type of monument

---

[72] Behold, the queen was a spark to our God
[73] Or: (Behold, for my creeping (for my disappearance), this is with thyme with its seven walls)

# Chapte 6

# Sabai and Geez inscription

# 21– Sabai inscription from Saudi Arabia[74]

This is one of the inscriptions unearthed in southern Arabia. There is a fracture on the right side and perhaps on the left as well. The publisher did not specify the date of these engravings.

---

[74] AWOL – The Ancient world online
https://ancientworldonline.blogspot.com/2010/10/open-access-corpus-of-south-arabian.html

The inscription reads:

... (ي) و م / ذ ب ح / م د ه و و / ب ر ع ظ
... ر ق م / د ك د د / م د م د م د ك ذ ك

... (Y)  W M / Dh B H' / M D H W W / B R A'
z'

We read it in Syriac:

... ܩܡ / ܕܕܒ / ܡܕܘܘ / ܟܐ ܘܡܗܘ ܟܠ

Translation:
On the day when he sacrificed, Madhu and son Adh

# 22– Sabai inscription from Najran – Saudi Arabia[75]

Three gold rings, a bronze bull's head, and an inscription about seven and a half feet long, written in Sabaean, were found at the site of the groove. It dates back to the third century BC.
The inscription reads:

و ه ب ا ط / ب ن م ا ق ن / د ط و / ب ي ت ه و

''' ‬

W H B A G / B N M A Q N / D G W / B Y T
H W
When we read it in Arabic, it does not give meaning, so we will read it in Syriac:

'''

Translation:
Whab ag …son maqn in his house and

75 Ancient Inscription Uncovered in Saudi Arabia
https://www.archaeology.org/news/11255-230227-arabia-musnad-inscription

# 23– Sabai inscription from

# Maliha UAE[76]

An inscription of a tombstone from the site of Mleiha, dated by the French scholar Christian Gopin to the second century BC, is considered one of the most important inscriptions discovered in the UAE (according to the source), due to the writing it contains in the southern Musnad script. Christian says that it was written on the bricks before they dried.

---

[76] 24 newspaper, Saturday, November 15, 2014 /
Report: The UAE is a civilization written on rocks and its history is written in all its font
/https://24.ae/article/117979

But I believe that it was written on the outer cover of the grave whether it was made of clay or cement. It was studied by the French scientist Christian Gopin, and Gopin's reading was as follows:

The soul and grave of Ubaid - son Aws, whose daughter was sgamatke bint Shamattakbi - daughter Ashq Aws.

The reading of "Goban" means that "the owner of the grave is named Ubaidah son Aws, and the grave's daughter is Ghadana daughter Shamattakbi, daughter of Ashq Aws, and Goban interprets the name Ghadana as a feminine noun.

We will re-read what we can read, as the image of the inscription is not clear and there is difficulty in reading:

ن ف س
... د (ي) ص ط ... ا ط
... ت ن ن .. / ي ... ر ا ن ب
د ك ن ت هـ ... ت ش م ت
... ت .. ب ل ..
(د ق ر) ق ق ~
ﮪ � ᐳ ᐞ
ﮪ ᐞ ''' ﮊ ''' ᐞ ᐳ ᐝ

ᐝ

ﮪᐞ ᐞ ᐞ ''' ᐝ ﮪ

When we read it in Arabic, it does not give meaning, so we will read it in Syriac:

ﻗﻮ (ﺑﻮﻟ)

ᐞ ᐺ ᐞ ᐝ

ᵈᵘ ''' , ''' ᵢ ᴿᵇ

ᵈᵃᵉ ᵈᵢ ''' ᵐᵈᵘ ᵉᵧ

... ᵈᵢ ᵈᵃ '''

Translation:
Vote (fell) G built D…
Built R.. Swelled up…/ on fire … Swelled up
His tumor was cleansed... T named T…
… Heart T…

# 24– Inscription from the site of Dibba Al–Hisn – UAE[77]

An incense burner, or perhaps part of a jar, was found at the site of Dibba Al-Hisn - Emirates. It is decorated in a

---

feminine shape and geometric ornaments are painted in red in ribbon decorations. It dates back to the first century AD and perhaps later (according to the source). It has writing on the right side in the Sabaean script.

The inscription reads:

ر ت ن خ ن هـ ك ك ن

R T N KH  H K N
When we read it in Arabic, it does not give meaning, so we will read it in Syriac:

Translation:
Move nkha, withheld
Or: Move the base

# 25– Funerary tablet, from the necropolis of Amud UAE[78]

A bilingual funerary inscription in Mleiha - Sharjah. The outer frame is in Aramaic and the inner inscription is in Sabaean. Some believe that it dates back to the third century BC (215 BC). However, Professor Issa says that it dates back to the end of the third century AD.

The frame is written in Aramaic, and there is difficulty reading some of its letters, especially the lower side and part of the left side, as they are erased. It seems to me that

---

[78] History of the United Arab Emirates
https://en.wikipedia.org/wiki/History_of_the_United_Arab_Emirates
**and:**
https://aip.ae/project.php?id=82

the writing is on the cover of the grave or the facade, whether it is made of clay or cement. When I return to reading the researcher Issa Yusuf, it turns out that his reading of the inscription was incorrect, as it is an interpretation of what He saw.

Aramaic text reads:
Topside :

ن ح ن ع ن ي م ب ر م ع م ي ط ب ه ع م ي و

N H' N A' N Y M B R M A' M Y G B H A' M Y W
The left side:

ش ن ت ...

SH N T ...
Bottom side: …..
The right sid:

و ط و ب و ز م و ش ف ...

 W G W B W Z M W SH F...
When we read it in Arabic, it does not give clear meaning, so we will read it in Syriac:

ܥܝܠ ‘‘‘

. . . . . . .

ܘ ܐܠܟ ܒܟܘܡ ܗܩܘ ‘‘‘

Translation:
Arranged, pity and sang m but with yagbi with yo
Year …
And the mast, ringing, and crawling
 Or:

ܗ ܟܬܐ ܡܠܟܝ ܟܐ ܟܬܟ ܙ ܟܠ ܡ ܚܠ ܝ ܠ

ܥܝܠ ‘‘‘

‘‘‘

ܘ ܐܠܟ ܙ ܡ ܘ ܗ ܩ ܥ ‘‘‘

Translation:
Arranged, pity and sang m but with yagbi with yo
Year …
And in the south of m and crawl
Regarding the Sabaean writing inside the square, there
is a distortion in lines 3,4,5, which makes it difficult to
read:

ن ف س / و ق ب ر ر / ع م د / ب ن/
ط ر /ب ن / ع ط ي / ب ق ر / م ط ب
ع م ن / ا ذ ي / ب ن ي / ع „ ب / ب ر
ي / ع م ذ ...
ب ق ر / ...

ܠ ܗܙܟܕܡܡܘܘܩ ܠ ܝ ܙ ܟ ܡ ܩ ܟ ܗ ܝ ܠ

ܠ ܗ ܝ ܙ ܟ ܠ ܠ ܟ ܩ ܡ ܝ ܗ ܙ ܟ ܠ

ܠ ܩ ܠ ܗ ܙ ܩ , ܠ ܟ ܙ , ‘‘‘ ܟ ܗ ܙ ,

, ܠ ܩ ܗ

N F S / W Q B R / A' M D / B N[79]
G R / B N / A' G Y / B Q R / M G B
A' M N / DH Y / B N Y / A' .. B / B R
Y / A' M DH ...
B Q R / ...

Reading the inscription in both Arabic and Syriac does not give a clear meaning due to distortion. However, we will read it in Syriac as well, since the meaning is a little clearer.

ܢܦܫ ܘܩܒܪ ܐܡܕ ܒܢ

ܓܪ ܒܢ ܐܓܝ ܒܩܪ ܡ ܓܒ

ܐܡܢ ܕܝ ܒܢܝ ܐ ''' ܒ ܒܪ

ܝ ܐܡܕ

ܒܩܪ

Translation:
The soul[80] and grave of Amad son
Gar son of Age, ask M next to
With us, this is sons A...B sons,
Y Baptize
Asked

---

# 26– Inscription from Al–Sawda – Yemen[81]

It was found on the site called (Al-Sawda). It dates back to the seventh century BC, as acknowledged by the committee. Its writing is clear in the picture, so I read it simply.

The committee read it:

ي د ع ا ب / م ل ك / ن ش ن / س ح د ث / ب

، د ح ك د ل م ح ح ح م د د ه د ب ،،،

Y D A' A B / M L K / N SH N / S H' D TH /B
We read it in Syriac:

[81] United Nations Educational, Scientific and Cultural Publications - Social Fund for Development - National Museum in Sana'a / Collection of inscriptions from the sites of Al-Jawf, Part 2 - Munir Arish and the Frenchman Remy Audoin - Sana'a 2007

''' ܥܬ ܐܟ ܟܠܝܟ ܝܤ ܣܘܡ ܢܕܬ ܒ '''

translation:
The king nashan's father know kindness of B…

OR:

Yadaab the king of Nashan kindness the rule b..

The meaning is clear, but it seems to me that there is a break in the inscription. It is unreasonable for the writer to write the letter (b) alone, so there must be a continuation of the word.

United Nations Educational, Scientific and Cultural Publications - Social Fund for Development - National Museum in Sana'a / Collection of inscriptions from the sites of Al-Jawf, Part 2 - Munir Arish and the Frenchman Remy Audoin - Sana'a 2007.

# 27– Inscription from Ethiopia and Eritrea[82]

A piece of pottery, written in the Ge'ez script. It has a fracture on the right and left. Dates back 3rd to 4th Centuries.

What is striking is the use of the sign (=) at the right beginning of the writing and in the middle. This means that it may have been an arithmetic symbol with the sign ,(+)a piece of pottery written in the Ge'ez script, with a division on the right and left. What is striking is the use of the sign (=) at the right beginning of the writing and in the middle. This means that it may have been an arithmetic symbol with a sign (+).

---

https://x.com/Erihistory/status/1297444233578569729[82]

Also, the last letter may be the letter (t) and may be an image of the cross compared to the fourth letter from the left, which looks like a sign (+).

The inscription is read from left to right:

If the first symbol (T)  it is read in Arabic :

ت و ا ت ف ض ك = ب ش ف ح

ܬ ܗ ܟܐ ܗܩ ܢۑ ܢ = ܒ ܥܩ ܗ ܢ ...

؏ T W A T F D' K = B SH F H'
When we read it in Arabic, it does not give a clear meaning, so we will read it in Syriac:

ܬܗ ܟܐ ܗܩ ܢۑ ܢ = ܒ ܥܩ ܗ ܢ ...

Translation:
Move the waterwheel D'K = B crawling H'
 If the first symbol  ( ؏)
it is read:

و ا ت ف ض ك = ب ش ف ح

ܗ ܟܐ ܗܩ ܢۑ ܢ = ܒ ܥܩ ܗ ܢ

W A T F D' K = B S H T H'
If the first symbol is read as a cross, it is read in Syriac:

ܗ ܟܐ ܗܩ ܢۑ ܢ = ܒ ܥܩ ܗ ܢ

Translation:
And came fd'k = B crawling H'

But if we consider it an arithmetic symbol, it will be:
597= 490. According to what the Syriac letters symbolize
1443= 707. According to what the Geez letters symbolize
Perhaps because of the fraction, the equation is incorrect.

# 28– Engraving by Cotard[83]

Graffiti on the walls, from the site of Dukhanamu, Kotar (near Asmara), dates back to the 8th-7th century BC. They are in the Geez and Sabaean script. This is an indication that the Sabaean script may have originated in Abyssinia, or perhaps also that this writing is in the stage of the development of the Sabaean script to Jeezy or vice versa.

The writing is not clear as it was engraved on an irregular stone, that is, in the form of a block, so there was difficulty in writing, or perhaps the writer was a primitive student.

The first line is read from left to right and has damage on both sides:

---

[83] HAL Id:halshs-
https://shs.hal.science/halshs-00865945

The inscription reads:

... و ك ي م ...
‘‘‘ ۄ ، ۄۯ ، ۲ ‘‘‘

... W K Y M ...
Maybe it is:

ܚܟܡܬܐ

(H'KEMA ) Meaning (wise)

OR :

ܚܟܬܐ

Meaning: chandelier
Or maybe it's Kim's name
The second line from right to left contains unreadable
letters:

... ح (ص) ... و ح ت ن ل م س ب
‘‘ ۯ (ي) ‘‘‘ ۄ ۯ ۵ ۮ ل ۲ ۿ ۳ ت

... H'(S') ... W H'T N L M S B
When we read it in Arabic, it does not give clear
meaning, so we will read it in Syriac:

‘‘ (ي) ‘‘‘ ܘ ܗ ܠ ܕ ܡ ܗ ܬ

… S' … And fixed NL in the middle B …

OR:

.. ꝏ (ꙏ) ''' ꜚꞅꝏ ꞁ ꝏꞅ ꝏ

H'(S') … was circumcised L In the middle B…

or:

'' ꝏ (ꙏ) ''' ꜚꞅꝏ ꞁꞁ ꝏꞅ ꝏ

And fix the middle with

or:

.. ꝏ (ꙏ) ''' ꜚꞅꝏ ꞁ ꝏꞅ ꝏ

He circumcised the middle with
The third line reads:

...ح ت / ب ن ,,,<br>''' ꞁ ꝏ ꞁ ꝏ '''

… H'T / BN…
Maybe it is:

ꝏ ꞁ ꜚꞅ

H'T L B N
Meaning:
Firm our heart

# 29– Inscription from Goa Temple[84]

[84] Proceedings of the seminar for arabian studies Volume 40 2010
https://www.researchgate.net/profile/Pawel-
Wolf/publication/261510810_The_Almaqah_Temple_of_Meqaber_Ga'ewa_ne
ar_Wuqro_TigrayEthiopia/links/0deec5346fa639d15e000000/The-Almaqah-
Temple-of-Meqaber-Gaewa-near-Wuqro-Tigray-Ethiopia.pdf

This relief is in the National Museum - Addis Ababa[85], and it is a statue of a seated woman and several incense burners around her. The writing on the statue says, as the source claims:

"Because he (God) gives a child to the Yamanat

It was discovered near the Temple of Gawa, and according to researcher Addi Gelemo  (RIE 52)[86] the inscription dates back to the seventh or eighth century BC—placing it within the period of the Kingdom of Damat.

The inscription is written in Musnad script. It contains a break, and the first line begins with two commas (|), and there are other commas in the first and second lines.

The first line is read from left to right according to the direction the letter is drawn, while the second line starts from right to left.

The inscription reads:

اطمق هـ|طوك ||

يمن ت/وطدم /

---

A G M Q H / G W K /
Y M N T / W G D M /
When we read it in Arabic, it does not give a clear
meaning, so we will read it in Syriac:

Translation:
Pond is tired in K ..
A sea that rose and crashed
OR:
The flood tired, screamed
A sea that rose and crashed

# 30 – Bronze cauldron[87]

A bronze cauldron, the writing on its outer surface may be a religious spell. The writing is free of space.

 It was published by J. Gebre Selassie in 2011, and the source says that it dates back to the civilization of Demet, that is, before the third century BC.

Reading:

.. ت ب ع ك ذ ر خ ي ...

‘‘‘, ⲥ⳦ⲓ ⲥ ⲍ ⲃ ⲏ

---

... T B A' K R DH KH Y ...
In Syriac, meaning:

ܗܟ݂ܐ ܚ݂ ܕ݁ܚ ''' 

Track where it purified

OR:

Track the location of the washing

# 31- Sabai inscription from H'aqna – Somalia[88]

An inscription in Musnad script from the Haqna region, the eastern coast of Somalia. It is similar to the Ethiopic-Eritrean inscriptions, written in the manner of a plow. The original inscription is unclear and has breaks on both sides.

Reading:

The first line from right to left:

ط ح ت / ب ن / ز ا د م / ع ب د / ب ن / ح ن ف ر م / هـ ق ن
ي

---

[88] Sabaeans on the Somali coast
Alessia Prioletta1 , Christian Julien Robin, Jérémie Schiettecatte, Iwona Gajda, Khaldūn H azzāʿ N uʿmān5
and:
Riad Al-Farah, quoted by Mr. Mahdi Saeed
/https://ralfareh.blogspot.com/2022/12/musnadsomal.html

G H'T / B N / Z A D M / A' B D / B N / H'N F R M / H
Q N Y

The second line from left to right:

A KH KH T N / M A' S L T N / W (A') B N H W / F
R Z N M / Y O M
Third line from left to right:

R SH W / A KH KH T N / B R H'B M / T'(B) M B N
Y / S L M T M
When we read it in Arabic, it does not give clear
meaning, so we will read it in Syriac:



---

Translation:
G confirmed that Ibn Zadam Abd Ibn Hanfarm Haqni
Akhkhten crushed smoke and his son Farznam the day
 His head is like flax, and it shines brightly
When compared to another version published on the
website[91] (Tawfiq Al-Sami'i / Al-Harf 28 newspaper
published on Sunday 3/12/2023 , Show me reads:

ح ت / ب ن / ت ن ق د م / و ب د / ب ن / ح ن ف ر م / ه ـ ق ن ي
ا خ خ ت ن / م و ز (س) ل ت ن / و ب ن ي .. و/ف ر ت ن م / ن ع م
ر ش و / ا خ خ ت ن / ب ر ح ب م/ذ م ب ن س/ل م ت م

H' T / B N / T N Q D M / W B D / B N / H' N F R M /
H Q N Y
A KH KH T N / M W Z (S) L T N / W B N Y .. W / F R
T N M / N A' M
R SH W / A KH KH T N / B R H" B M / DH M B N S /
L M T M
When we read it in Arabic, it does not give clear
meaning, so we will read it in Syriac:

<hr>

91
https://www.facebook.com/Hayelaluby/photos/a.102980951758941/42040601
3349765

Translation:

Make sure Ibn Ten is in front of and.. The son Hanfarm H acquired

Akhkhtn vile Tin and family...T ran away and slept the day

Crush (knowledge) Akhkhten son Hibbam blooding, son Salam completed

The difference is slight, and this means that either the two inscriptions are different, or the writer made a mistake in one of them and tried to correct in the second.

# 32– Sabai inscription from Bunland – Somalia[92]

An inscription from the coastal region of the state of Bunland, near the city of Qandala in Somalia, located in the heart of the Bree land.

It has fractures on both sides and deformation at the bottom (the right side). And the writing in it is in the plowing style.

[92] https://www.researchgate.net/figure/Inscription-Bari-2021-3-Courtesy-Mahad-Jebiy_fig6_356347086
and : HAL
https://shs.hal.science/halshs-04135613v1/file/2021%20Robin%20Pioletta%20Schiettecatte%20et%20al%20OCRAI%20Sabe%CC%81ns%20dans%20la%20Corne%20Afrique%20Somalie.pdf

The inscription reads:

م ل ك ن / ب ن / ن ع م / ع ر ب / ا خ خ
ت ن / ه ق ن ي / ا خ خ ت ن / ن ف س ن ...
.. و م / م ي ر / ب ع م / ا ب ه و ط م
.. ر ... ي .. ن ب / ع ث ي ه ي / ب ...

ܡ ܠ ܝ ... ... ... ... ...
... ... ... ... ...
''' ... ... ... ... ...
''' ... ... ''' ... ''' ' ''' ... ''

M L K N / B N / N A' M / A' R B / A KH KH
T N / H Q N Y / A KH KH T N / N F S N ..
.. W M / M Y R / B A' M / A B H W T' M
.. R ... Y .. N B / A' TH Y H Y / B ..

In Arabiq it means:
Our king son of Naam Arab akhkh..
Tn h qne Akhkhtn Our soul ..
… WM Mer by uncle Abho T'M
.. R .. Y .. NB .. A'THY HYB ..

When we read it in Arabic, it does not give clear
meaning, so we will read it in Syriac:

ܡ ܠ ܝ ... ... ... ... ...
... ... ... ... ...
''' ... ... ... ... ...
''' ... ... ''' ... ''' ' ''' ... ''

Translation:

Our king preached and sang the Arabs of Akkhtan
H Akhkhten bought our lot
… And Memyar by his father Tam
.. R … Y … NB .. B wronged B..
The meaning is incomplete due to the breakage and the
difficulty of reading some letters.

# The sources

1- Cuneiform - World History Encyclopedia
/https://www.worldhistory.org/cuneiform
2- The Cuneiform Writing System in Ancient
Mesopotamia: Emergence and Evolution
https://edsitement.neh.gov/lesson-plans/cuneiform-
writing-system-ancient-mesopotamia-emergence-and-
evolution
3- GETTING STARTED WITH... SUMERIAN
 BY PATRICK J. BURNS
https://isaw.nyu.edu/library/blog/getting-started-with-
sumerian
4- **Ugaritic** alphabet writing system
Written and fact–checked by the editors of
Encyclopaedia Britannica
https://www.britannica.com/topic/Ugaritic-alphabet
5- Ugarit and the Origins of Alphabet - NATASHA
SHELDON
     https://historyandarchaeologyonline.com/ugarit-and-
the-origins-of
6- New archaeological discovery in Jerusalem adds to
evidence of the great biblical king's reign.
BY BRENT NAGTEGAAL
https://www.thetrumpet.com/20703-king-josiah-proved-
again
7- NEWS & NOTES
T H E O R I E N T A L I N S T I T U T E
NO. 207 FALL 2010 © THE ORIENTAL INSTITUTE
OF THE UNIVERSITY OF CHICAGO
The Origins of Writing in Mesopotamia
Christopher Woods

https://www.academia.edu/16554752/The_Origins_of_
Writing_in_Mesopotamia?email_work_card=thumbnail
8- THE CONCEPTION AND DEVELOPMENT OF
THE EGYPTIAN WRITING SYSTEM
ELISE V. MACARTHUR

9- THE STORY OF THE EARLY ALPHABET
JOSEPH LAM
10- JOURNAL OF THE
INSTITUTE OF ARCHAEOLOGY
OF TEL AVIV UNIVERSITY
Published by Taylor & Francis
For the Emery and Claire Yass Publications in
Archaeology of
The Institute of Archaeology of Tel Aviv University
TEL AVIV
11- Sabaeans on the Somali coast
Alessia Prioletta1, Christian Julien Robin, Jérémie
Schiettecatte, Iwona Gajda, Khaldūn H azzāʿ N uʿmān5
12- History of writing
From Wikipedia, the free encyclopedia #
Writing_materials
https://en.wikipedia.org/wiki/History_of_writing
13- The Evolution of Writing
Published in James Wright, ed., INTERNATIONAL
ENCYCLOPEDIA OF SOCIAL AND BEHAVIORAL
SCIENCES, Elsevier, 2014
https://sites.utexas.edu/dsb/tokens/the-evolution-of-
writing/
14- DEVELOPMENT OF WRITING IN THE
ANCIENT WORLD
https://africame.factsanddetails.com/article/entry-
63.html

15- An ancient Aramaic inscription from western Iran /
Prof. Dr. Farouk Ismail - Professor at the Free
University of Berlin
Journal of the Saudi Society for Archaeological Studies
- Studies in the World of Archeology and Heritage -
Issue February 2020

# The biography

+ Nazar Hanna Yousif Dayraya
+Birthplace and date of birth: Derabun - Zakho 1956
+ Academic achievement:
Bachelor's degree in Management and Economics - Al-Mustansiriya University
Cultural activity
Since the seventies, he has been working in the cultural community, where he has held several administrative positions in these institutions:
+ Member of the Cultural Association for Syriac - Speakers since 1976 / Member of the Administrative Board for the years 1977-1981
+ Member of the Syriac Writers' Union since 1977 / Member of the Administrative Board in 1979. President of the Syriac Writers' Union since 2003-2010
+ Member of the General Union of Iraqi Writers since 1983. Deputy Secretary-General of the Union of Writers in Iraq from 2004 to 2010.
+ Member of the Arab Writers Union since 1985
+ Secretary General of the Writers Club in Iraq in the nineties
+ Member of the Administrative Board of the Ashur Panipal Association - Chairman of the Cultural Committee since 1994 and for two consecutive terms.
+ Member of the Cultural Committee of the Antonine Hormuzticism Order from 1994-2007.
+ Founding member of the Central Board of the Yunnan Hozaya Center for Future Studies.

+ Member of the Australian-Arab Cultural Forum –
Australia
+ He worked as a member of the editorial staff of
magazines:
(Qala Soryaya, Syriac Writers, Rabnutha, and the Iraqi
writer).
+He received several shields and certificates of
appreciation from Iraq, Syria, Lebanon, Egypt, Jordan,
Kuwait, Australia,
(Morocco, Sweden).
+ He received the Charbel Baini Award for the year
2015, which is awarded by the Alphabet Institute in the
historic Lebanese city of Byblos, on behalf of the Media
Alienation Foundation in Australia.
+ He received the Golden Jubilee Shield from the Union
of Syriac Writers and Authors in 2023.
+ He participated in many festivals, conferences, and
seminars inside and outside Iraq.
+ He had media columns in the Behra (paper)
newspaper and in some media and cultural sites,
electronic like newspaper Ainkawa.com..
+ He had many cultural episodes on the satellite channel
(Ashur and Ishtar), and many interviews were
conducted with him on television (Ashur, Ishtar, Al-
Hurra, Nour Al-Sharq, Subara, Maryam, Erisat),
electronic media stations, newspapers, and several radio
stations.


+ Published research
+ In addition to dozens of poems and dozens of articles
published in newspapers and magazines that were
published in Iraq or outside Iraq, and dozens of articles

and poems in electronic newspapers. The author published the following research:

1- Folkloric paintings from our beloved north / Qala Suriya magazine, latest issue.
2- Repetition in contemporary Syriac poetry / Syriac Writers Magazine.
3- Are the Muwashahat of Andalusian origin or Syriac - in Syriac / Rabnutha Magazine.
4- The Epic of Qatini - in Syriac / Assyria Bulletin.
5- The national feeling among the rulers of Orhai - in Syriac / Rabnutha Magazine.
6- Monasticism in the Thought of Aphrahat / Rabnutha Magazine.
7- The monastery between the tragedy of life and the search for happiness (a study of Nazik al-Malaika's poem) / Rabnutha Magazine.
8- Culture as understood by anthropologists / Rabnotha Magazine.
9- Determining the history of the Songs of Solomon based on their poetic form / Rabnutha Magazine.
10- Death and resurrection in the poems of Badr Shaker Al-Sayyab / Christian Thought Magazine.
11- Abgar's letter to Christ between truth and fiction / - Spirit Harp Magazine.
12- Are the Muwashahat of Andalusian origin or Syriac (in Arabic) / Banipal Magazine.
13- Poetry's weights according to Al-Khalil, are they authentic or imported? / Iraqi Writer Magazine.
14- Other research within Syriac literature conferences.
15- Several studies and translations in Radya Chaldea Magazine, Nohadra Magazine, Sefrotha Magazine,

Najm Beit Nahrin Magazine, Babylon Magazine, and websites.
Other special publications for Syriac literature conferences in Iraq, Egypt, Syria, Lebanon, and Australia…

Publications (53) author:

(Poetry collections 14, literary and critical studies 16, translations 15, miscellaneous 4). As well as (3) ready to print.

Poetry collections:

1- Martyr from Derabun / Al-Hawadith Press, 1984, in Syriac.

2- Rain is a Melody of Memories / Atlas Press 1986 - in Syriac and Arabic.

3- The Struggle of Existence / published by the Iraqi Writers Union, 1994 - in Syriac and Arabic.

4- A Vacant Seat / Yarmouk Press, 2001 - in Syriac.

5- For Whom Do the Birds Sing? Yarmouk Press 1999 - Poetry for children.

6- Hot Conflict / Syriac, published by the Ministry of Culture in the Kurdistan Region.

7- All the Earth is equal in view of the Wises / Syriac language - published by the Syriac Writers Union - and at the expense of the Office of the Minister of Finance, Mr. Sarkis Aghajan - Publishing Department.

8- Thus Spoke Kyasa / Syriac language, published by the Ashurian Cultural Center, Dohuk, 2015.

9- Scattered Papers - First Collection / Electronic Publishing - Poetry Collection in Arabic 2016.

10- Scattered Papers - second Collection / Electronic Publishing - Poetry Collection in Arabic 2016.

11- Scattered Papers - third Collection / Electronic
Publishing - Poetry Collection in Arabic 2016.
12- Navel, grass and immortality / 2017 Enheduanna
Center, Cambridge – Britain.
13- This cradle is not my cradle / a collection of poetry
in Syriac - Australia - Melbourne 2021.
14- The Journey of Gilgamesh and his struggle with
Humbaba - Syriac Arabic / Melbourne 2024.

Literary studies

1- The Golden meters in Syriac Poetry / Al-Yarmouk
Press 1989.
2- Our contemporary poem (the poem of the twentieth
century) / first edition, Yarmouk Press 1998, the 2nd
edition with its new additions/ Erbil Al-Dabbagh Press
2018.
3- Rhythm in Poetry - A Comparative Study between
Syriac and Arabic - / Special Edition of the Symposium
(Between Arabic and Syriac - The Iraqi Scientific
Academy) 1997, and then printed as a book by the
Yarmouk Press in 2000, the 2nd edition, Beirut, Jameel
Press for Printing and Distribution 2017.
4- Letter from Mara Ben Sarafyoun / 1st edition,
published by the Iraqi Scientific Academy, 2002, the
2nd edition, published by Al-Sayeh Library, Trablos
(Tripoli) - Lebanon, 2017.
5- Highlights on the History of Syriac Literature / in
Arabic - from publications of the House of Cultural
Affairs - Ministry of Culture, Baghdad 2007, the 2nd
edition, with its new additions - entitled (The role of
Syriacs in the scientific and literary renaissance,
especially in the Umayyad and Abbasid eras) Australia
2021.

6- Landmarks of modernity in Syriac poetry / Kurdish Directorate of Culture and Publishing - Baghdad 2014 Iraqi Ministry of Culture.

7- The missing links in the history of poetry and its metres (a comparative study between Syriac, Arabic, Kurdish, and other neighboring languages) / New Hope House, Syria, Damascus 2016, the 2nd edition, Australia 2021.

8- A reading of contemporary Syriac poetry / a critical study - Beirut - Jameel Printing and Distribution Press 2019.

9- The Origins of Syriac and Arabic Writing / Publications by Al-Farabi Publishing and Distribution House - Lebanon 2019.

10- Readings in Contemporary Lebanese Literature and Art / 1st Edition Australia 2021, the 2nd Edition Dar Fikrat Com for Distribution and Publishing - Algeria - Ouargla 2023.

11- A Syriac reading of the inscriptions discovered in the Arabian Peninsula and Yemen / Abjad Foundation for Translation, Publishing and Distribution - Iraq Babylon 2022.

12- A Syriac reading of the inscriptions discovered in the Iraqi city of Hadra / Abjad Foundation for Translation, Publishing and Distribution - Iraq Babylon 2022.

13- A Syriac reading of the inscriptions discovered in the Syrian city of Palmyra / Abjad Foundation for Translation, Publishing and Distribution - Iraq Babylon 2022.

14- Readings on poetry and fine art / published by the General Union of Writers and Authors in Iraq – 2022.

15- A Syriac reading of the inscriptions discovered in Ethiopia and Eritrea, first edition, Australia 2024.

16- Diving and sailing into the depths of literary texts (Arabic and Syriac) - General Union of Writers in Iraq 2025.

17- The origins of writing from Sumerian to Aramaic, Sabaean, and Geezy / soon.

Translation

1- From modern Arabic poetry / published by the Mar Gorgis Cultural Center - Baghdad 2003.

2- From contemporary Arabic poetry - translation / from publications of the Union of Syriac Writers and at the expense of Dar Al-Hadaf for Printing, Media and Publishing.

3- In the beginning was the conflict / a collection of poetry - translation from Syriac to Arabic / published by the Department of Cultural Affairs, Baghdad, 2013 - Ministry of Culture within the Baghdad Capital of Arab Culture project.

4- The Lebanese poet Charbel Baaini and the sufferings of immigration - translation of poems from Arabic into Syriac / published by the Al-Gharaba Foundation - Australia - first edition 2015 - second edition 2020.

5- Death and Birth by the poet Ibrahim Yalda / translation from Syriac to Arabic / Beirut 2017 - Jameel Press for Printing and Distribution.

6- From contemporary Iraqi poetry / Al-Dabbagh Press - Erbil 2018.

7- From the beginning there was the navel, the grass, and eternity - translation from Syriac into Arabic / Beirut 2018 in limited quantity.

8- Baidar the Contemporary Poem (Lebanon - Syria) / published by the Syriac Cultural Center of the Syriac Association - Lebanon 2019.

9- Baidar, the very contemporary short story (Lebanon - Syria)/ Al-Jamil Press, Beirut 2019.

10- From Australian poetry for children - translation from English to Arabic - / Lulu Printing and Publishing Company – 2022.

11- From Australian poetry for children - translation from English to Syriac - / Lulu Printing and Publishing Company – 2022.

12- Excerpts from the Contemporary Arabic Short Story Kindergarten / published by the Union of Syriac Writers – 2022.

13- Excerpts from the Kindergarten of Contemporary Arabic Poetry / published by the Syriac Writers Union – 2022.

14- T. s Eliot the Great Poet / Publications of the Ministry of Culture - Directorate of Syriac Culture and Arts - Erbil 2023.

15- What will the immigrant carry in his bag of ?/ memories
Manhal Al-Quraa, Publishing House - Syria - Aleppo 2024, with the support of the Hume City Council.

16- The origins of writing from Sumerian to Aramaic (Syriac, Arabic, Hebrew), Sabaean, and Geezy / in your hands.


Sporadic

1- The Way of the Cross - in Syriac - paraphrased - / from the publications of the Mar Gorgis Cultural Center - Baghdad 2003.

2- Derabun between past and present / Mar Gorgis Cultural Center.
3- Syriac hymns - in Syriac / electronic publication.
4- An Anthology of Syriac Poetry (by subscription) / Publications of the Syriac Writers Union - Iraq - Erbil 2019.

Ready to print

1- My diary.
2- A collection of articles in literature